ROBOCOP 2 ™

A **Jon Davison** PRODUCTION ● AN **Irwin Kershner** FILM

Peter Weller ● **Nancy Allen** ● "**Robocop_2**"

Daniel O'Herlihy ● **Tom Noonan** ● **Belinda Bauer** ● **Gabriel Damon**

DIRECTOR OF PHOTOGRAPHY **Mark Irwin** ● VISUAL EFFECTS BY **Phil Tippett**

ROBOCOP DESIGNED BY **Rob Bottin** ● MUSIC BY **Leonard Rosenman**

EXECUTIVE PRODUCER **Patrick Crowley**

BASED ON CHARACTERS CREATED BY **Edward Neumeier** & **Michael Miner**

STORY BY **Frank Miller** ● SCREENPLAY BY **Frank Miller** & **Walon Green**

PRODUCED BY **Jon Davison**

DIRECTED BY **Irwin Kershner**

Novel by Ed Naha
Screenplay by Frank Miller & Walon Green
Story by Frank Miller
Based on characters created by
Edward Neumeier & Michael Miner

J

JOVE BOOKS, NEW YORK

ROBOCOP 2

A Jove Book / published by arrangement with
Creative Licensing Corporation

PRINTING HISTORY
Jove edition / June 1990

ISBN: 0-515-10410-8

Jove Books are published by The Berkley Publishing Group,
200 Madison Avenue, New York, New York 10016.
The name "JOVE" and the "J" logo
are trademarks belonging to Jove Publications, Inc.

PRINTED IN THE UNITED STATES OF AMERICA

10 9 8 7 6 5 4 3 2 1

For the Gab
and the gifts she brought

PART ONE

"This world is a comedy for those who think . . . and a tragedy for those who feel."

—Horace Walpole

1

He was a cop.

A good cop.

His name had been Murphy once, Alex Murphy, back when he had been a man. But time and circumstances had changed all that. Now he was something *more* than a man, and something less, as well.

"The Future of Law Enforcement," he was called. A being part human, part machine that had been programmed to serve the populace.

His world could be summed up quite succinctly, thanks to the expertise of the robotics technicians who'd pulled his bullet-riddled human body back from the brink of death and housed its remnants in a powerful metal shell.

Directive One: Serve the public trust.

Directive Two: Uphold the law.

Directive Three: Protect the innocent.

The lights of Old Detroit twinkled across Robo-Cop's face visor as he guided his TurboCruiser down one of the countless pockmarked, half-deserted streets of town. Crumbling shells of buildings were nestled next to stores and tenements still struggling to survive, their neon lights buzzing spastically, their doorways hanging from their hinges. Large metal gates were everywhere, put up by tenants and shop owners to keep out the lowlifes. A futile effort, thought RoboCop. The tide of miscreants was surging. The city was being consumed by a virtual tidal wave of crime.

He pulled his TurboCruiser to a halt and climbed outside.

He gazed up at the full moon peeking through the soot and smog that caressed the city from above.

The moon glowed a sickly, green hue.

"It's made of green cheese, Daddy," he heard a little boy's voice call from the back of his mind. The being that was half-Murphy and half-robotics fought back a pang of hurt. He had had a son, once. A wife. A home. He'd lost all that when he became the first and only cyborg law-enforcement officer.

He was still trying to get the inner workings of his new self and his old self to jibe, to mesh.

There were times when the loneliness he experienced made him wince.

He was the only one of his kind.

What was more, he knew it.

RoboCop marched up to a nearly empty bar and peeked inside. A bartender dozed under a blaring television screen. Robo paused in the doorway, impervious to the smell of liquor and urine that arose from the gin mill. He gazed at the TV.

On the screen sat a parked car. A car thief resembling a weasel sidled up to the deserted vehicle and deftly slid a metal rod between the window and the door. Click. The lock gave way. The thief scrambled into the auto and took his place behind the wheel, a satisfied grin on his sweaty face.

Without warning, the car's safety belt slammed across the thug's chest like an angry tentacle. The thief continued to smile. What would they think of next? he seemed to chuckle. Then other tentacles appeared. Snap. Snap. Snap. They whipped across his chest and legs, binding him tightly to the front seat. The thief thrashed about helplessly, his eyes wide with terror.

The dashboard of the car *burrrped* to life. "You have just jimmied the wrong lock," it announced. "Welcome to the latest in family car defense."

RoboCop snorted as electrical flashes cascaded along the car's windows and down the extended straps. The thief uttered a muffled scream and passed out, his nervous system twitching violently from the high-voltage surge.

A cheerful pitchman, dressed like a used-car salesman, only worse, stepped up to the car and flung open the front door. The pan-fried body of the thief tumbled out onto the ground as the tentacles went back into hiding.

"MagnaVolt." The spokesman beamed. "The final word in auto security. No embarrassing alarm noise to upset the neighbors. No need to trouble the police."

The pitchman stepped over the smoking body and slid behind the wheel of the car, turning on the ignition. "And it won't even run down your battery."

RoboCop watched as the commercial came to an end, the car and salesman driving off, majestically, down the well-lit street.

The screen shifted to another scene. The evening news. Two TV newscasters who had for years made a determined effort to demonstrate who used the most—and most highly advanced—toothpaste appeared. Jess Perkins, a bubble-headed blonde who wore her dresses like most cars wore paint jobs, was usually the winner, although Robo theorized that most male viewers were equally dazzled by the areas below her chin. Coming in a close second, however, was Casey Wong, a crew-cut Eurasian whose smile was wide enough to have it included on most maps of the Detroit area.

Behind the twosome, a videotape clip showed a raging inferno. In the foreground, tropical trees seemed to wither as if on cue.

"The Amazon Nuclear Power Facility has blown its stack," Casey announced, still wearing his mannequin smile. "As I speak, it's irradiating the world's largest rain forest. Environmentalists call it a disaster!"

"But don't they always?" Jess laughed.

The scene changed, and Robo's eyes narrowed as a familiar form shambled across the screen. The massive, mechanical form of the Enforcement Druid, Series 209, strode across a city street, getting one of its feet stuck in a pothole. The gigantic hunchbacked robot, its rounded torso wobbling on its two legs, whirled and swirled its arms

6

around, waving its twenty-millimeter cannon muzzles, as it tried to regain its balance.

"In national news today," Jess continued, "Attorney General Marcus approved the ED209 combat unit for deployment in five American cities, despite widespread complaints of malfunction. Casey?"

Jess flashed Casey a perky smile.

Casey was still wearing his last one. "The latest on Old Detroit's police strike after this special public-service announcement."

The next image to appear on the screen was that of a bearded man in what appeared to be an admiral's outfit. Caught by surprise, the surgeon general, E. Edward Edwards, put out his cigarette and faced the cameras, wheezing.

"Ladies and gentlemen," came an omniscient voice, "the surgeon general of the United States."

"My fellow Americans," the surgeon general said sternly, cigarette smoke still trickling from his nostrils, "a health crisis is upon us. . . . And only *you* can put a stop to it. A new 'designer drug' has already made hopeless addicts of *one* out of *ten* citizens in Detroit . . . and this drug is spreading like wildfire across the country."

The bearded man held up a small plastic device: a NUKE ampule. "On the streets and in the schoolyards, they call it NUKE. It doesn't cost much to buy one of these."

The surgeon general was replaced by an animated scene that had apparently been conceived by someone with a shaky hand and a bad hangover. Two large fingers squeezed a NUKE ampule. A small needle popped out of the plastic and embedded itself into a vein in the animated user's neck. Then a diagram showed the liquid shooting straight up the spinal cord, sending various sectors of the brain into dayglow dementia.

"It's true that it will make you feel strong," the surgeon general continued. "Confident. On top of the world. But beware. . . . While its long-term effects have yet to be determined, this much is known: NUKE is the single most addictive substance on the planet."

The surgeon general pointed to a small cage in which a white rat was rebounding off the walls like a tailed Super-Ball. "This rat received the equivalent of a single dose of NUKE only five hours ago. Its euphoria was short-lived. Now it suffers the hideous agony of NUKE withdrawal. Don't be like him. Don't let your children be like him. Don't take NUKE!"

The surgeon general sat back on his desk, nearly toppling over an ashtray. "Thanks. Have a pleasant today and a *great* tomorrow."

Robo continued to stare at the screen. Jess and Casey returned, with a large police badge superimposed on a screen behind them. Across the badge, in red, was the word STRIKE.

"After four months," Casey intoned, "all but a handful of our cops remain on strike, demanding better terms from OmniConsumerProducts—OCP— the corporation contracted by the city to finance and run the Detroit police department. Negotiations came to a complete stop today and the cops are angry about it."

The screen showed a tape of dozens of police officers picketing in front of the Old Detroit stationhouse.

A concerned older cop, his face heavily lined from years of duty on the mean streets, faced the cameras before him. "OCP cut our salaries *forty percent*. They've canceled our pensions. And now they won't even *talk* to us? God knows why, but they seem to *want* this strike! They *want* the city to tear itself *apart*!"

The dozing bartender awoke at that point and casually flicked off the television. RoboCop stood, framed by the moonlight, in the doorway. The bartender looked up.

"How's it goin', Robo?" the old man said, his voice more a sigh than a tone.

RoboCop nodded casually. "Same old stuff," he managed to say.

"Yeah." The bartender nodded. "Ain't it the truth? I tell ya, it's damned depressing watching the news. I lived here all my life and I've *never* seen things so bad. Kids, flyin' high on that dope stuff, carrying around more firepower than I ever seen in all my years in Vietnam. Kids who should be home squeezing their zits is squeezin' triggers instead. Bad for business, let me tell you that. Nobody around here will go out on the streets anymore, between the hopheads and the muggers—and now this police strike."

The bartender caught himself. "No offense, Robo."

"'None taken," RoboCop replied, clenching his jaw.

Robo turned to face the smog-laden night. "Have a nice evening, sir."

"Oh, yeah." The bartender smirked. "I should live that long."

Robo marched back to his waiting TurboCruiser, his insides churning. He fought back the anger. He attempted to suppress his frustration. Not only was *his* world—his world inside—coming apart at the seams, but *the* world—*everybody*'s world—seemed to be coming unglued.

He slid behind the wheel of his car.

He would postpone his introspection for another, more appropriate time.

Tonight, he was just a cop.

A cop with a job to do.

And *nobody* was going to prevent him from doing it.

2

A stretch limo prowled through the cavernous streets of Detroit. In the back seat, Mayor Cyril Kuzak was not a happy man. Young and black, he had been elected as one of the people—someone who had come up from the slums of Old Detroit and was striving for the top.

He was at the top now; but, somehow, he was still looking *up* at those higher up than he. He hated that.

He ran a finger across the lapels of his thousand-dollar suit. He had all the trappings of power but was now powerless. If that was supposed to be some sort of a joke, Mayor Kuzak didn't find it funny.

He glanced up at the night sky. In the distance, high atop a sleek, spiraling skyscraper, the OCP logo blazed above the sleepy city. Kuzak's limo headed in that direction.

The figure next to Kuzak in the back seat stirred. Well-attired, button-downed Councilman George Poulos cleared his throat, as if giving a signal to the mayor. Stop daydreaming. Get your mind on business.

Kuzak grunted back as the limo pulled up in front of the OCP headquarters. Outside the car, a few workers were hosing the graffiti off a dormant ED209. *Fucking killer trashcan*, the mayor bristled to himself. He turned to Poulos.

"Remember," he cautioned the councilman, "I'm not here to *beg*!"

Poulos had done this dance before. "Of course not."

"I'm here to demand action!" Kuzak declared, as if trying to convince himself. "I'm here to *get* action!"

The two men walked toward the cathedrallike entrance of the building and made their way to the elevators leading up to the chambers of the head of OCP: a silver-haired despot known to everyone as, simply, the Old Man.

As the elevator slid up its clear tubeway, Kuzak fumed. He had quite a few things to tell that old fart. Who the hell did he think he was, messing around with Kuzak's city? With the police? With the people?

The elevator door swung open. A young, fresh-faced executive named Johnson opened the door to the inner sanctum for the two men. Johnson grinned like the Cheshire cat. It was crisis time, but hell, he had been with the Old Man through many a crisis. In fact, he had been promoted due to his ability to stay uninvolved. Kuzak scowled as he walked into the room. The place resembled a high-tech version of a mead hall from the days of

Camelot. Damn if it wasn't big enough to go bowling in. Kuzak continued to frown as he quickly calculated the cost of the room. Probably cost more than he made in a goddamned year.

Johnson kept his grin intact.

"It hardly befits the *dignity* of my office that I have to come to *you*, Johnson," Kuzak muttered.

"My apologies for the slight inconvenience, Your Honor," Johnson said, smoothly.

Poulos rolled his eyes and followed Kuzak into the room. A poker-faced attorney, Holzgang, leaned against a desk. The Old Man sat in his throne of a chair, facing a massive window and gazing out on the sprawling city below. He didn't acknowledge either visitor's presence.

Kuzak was still playing hardball with Johnson. "Slight?" he said, amazed and angry. "Twenty minutes in crosstown traffic isn't so *slight*! Not when you're the *mayor* of a *major* American *city*!"

The Old Man let go with an exasperated sigh; Kuzak was oblivious to it. Poulos slid into a chair and faced Johnson. "Let's get to business, shall we?" he opened. "When are you going to start paying the cops so they'll get back to work?"

The reptilian lawyer slithered into the chair opposite Poulos. "We're not a charity. The city owes us more than thirty-seven million dollars."

The mayor's jaw dropped open with a crack. He eased himself into a nearby chair. "You've got to cut us some slack. . . ."

The lawyer shrugged. "A deadline's a deadline. Sorry."

"How are we supposed to raise that kind of

money with things the way they are?" Kuzak demanded.

The Old Man spun his chair around and faced the assemblage for the first time. There was a small sneer curling around his lips. "You aren't," he said, the sneer turning into a full-fledged smirk.

Kuzak glanced at Johnson. "What the hell is he talking about?"

"We don't expect you to pay," the Old Man stated, firmly.

Holzgang flipped open a file folder before him and held up a wad of papers. "I refer you to our contract, *Your Honor*: 'In the event of default, OCP shall have the uncontested right of foreclosure on all city assets.'"

Kuzak's Adam's apple began break-dancing. Poulos's face went white. He grabbed the papers from Holzgang's hands, gulped, and faced the mayor.

"You *signed* that? You *twit*!" he screamed.

Kuzak tried to hang tough. "Don't call me a twit. *I'm the mayor!*"

Holzgang deftly took the papers out of Poulos's trembling hands. He smiled at the mayor.

Kuzak was outraged. "You're saying that we miss *one* payment, and you can *foreclose*?"

Holzgang nodded. The Old Man was delighted with himself. "We can, and we will. We're taking Detroit private."

"You deliberately undermined our credit!" Kuzak said, seething.

"That was the easy part," Holzgang replied.

The dawn of understanding began to flicker in Kuzak's eyes. "And you engineered the police strike! You *bastards*! You *want* Detroit to collapse! Just so you can *raid* it like you would any other corporation!"

Johnson chuckled in the Old Man's direction. "I thought he'd never get it."

Kuzak was too angry to be frightened. "Do you know how many people are *dying* in the streets out there? You—you're nothing more than a pack of *murderers*!"

Holzgang cleared his throat. "I'd advise you to say nothing further. It might be actionable."

"This is *bullshit*!" exclaimed Kuzak, at top volume. He faced the Old Man. "And you're *senile*!"

Within an instant, Kuzak was on his feet, heading for the Old Man. The Old Man watched him impassively. Poulos grabbed the mayor and led him toward the door. "Settle down," he cautioned. "Let's just get out of here, huh?"

Kuzak allowed himself to be led away. "I'm okay. I'm okay."

He flashed his campaign-winning smile at the OCP trio. "Gentlemen? One last thing . . ." Kuzak lunged toward the Old Man again. "Fuck you! We'll sue your asses!"

Poulos yanked the mayor out of the room, leaving the Old Man chuckling from his throne. "Give it your best shot, Your Honor. Give it your best shot."

Johnson walked up to the Old Man as Holzgang gathered up the contract. "If I may say so, sir, you are making history here. This is a very bold move."

The Old Man turned his attention back to the city outside. "It's evolution, Johnson. Nothing more. It is the *future*. Bumbling elected officials have brought this country to its knees. Responsible private enterprise must raise it up again. This is my dream, Johnson. It shall be my legacy."

"Congratulations, sir," Johnson said, backing out of the room with Holzgang in tow. "It was a stroke of master planning, the work of a true visionary."

The Old Man nodded. "That goes without saying, Johnson."

The Old Man didn't notice the two men easing the door shut behind them. He continued to gaze out upon the city. It had been a great city once. And it would be great once again. He had always considered Detroit to be *his* city. And now, in reality, it would be just that.

His city . . . and his alone.

3

Far below the Old Man's OCP tower office, in the area of the city known as Old Detroit, all hell, on schedule, was breaking loose. It was a nightly occurrence, with the city's poorest and most hopeless preying upon each other in spasmodic fits of random violence and bloodlust.

With the sound of burglar alarms echoing down the streets behind her, an old bag lady wheeled a shopping cart down her block. The cart, with only three wheels fully working, housed the sum of her life: three dozen crushed cans, good for redemption at her neighborhood market on the morrow—if she made it through the night in one piece.

The woman clutched her well-worn handbag to her right side. It was all she had left to remind her of another time, another life. A time when she had been considered a *person*. A life when she had loved and been loved.

Now she was sinking in a quagmire of despair. She did all she could to keep herself afloat. Maggie her name had been, once. Names didn't enter her world any more.

The old woman stiffened as the sound of screeching car brakes sliced through her memories, cleaving them neatly. The car, filled with laughing, drunk teenagers, slammed into her grocery cart, sending the cart, the cans, and the old woman tumbling onto the hard, cold sidewalk. The car sped off, the teenagers howling with glee.

The old woman surveyed the scene from the sidewalk. She was in pain, yes; but it was the kind of pain she was used to. She slowly got to her feet. "Bastards," she muttered.

She glanced around helplessly, her treasured tin cans still twirling in the street. She made a furtive move to gather them. A blow from nowhere slammed into her stomach. The old woman doubled over, and a young thug in a long dirty trenchcoat wrenched the handbag from her side, breaking her shoulder in the process.

The woman collapsed, sobbing on the pavement, half hoping that the chill of this particular night would invade her heart and her bones and end her misery once and for all.

The thief—handbag tucked, football style, under his left arm—sprinted down a street, passing a row of laughing hookers—mini-skirted girls, barely out of their teens, wearing more paint than most Monets. The last hooker extended a fishnet-covered leg, sending the young thief tumbling.

The asshole cartwheeled into a stack of cardboard boxes. "Bitches!" he screamed, as his head slammed into the pavement, knocking him senseless.

The whores descended upon him like ghouls,

rifling through his pockets and the stolen handbag.

"Bitches," he moaned.

"Go call a cop," one ten-year-old hooker sneered.

The girl let out an excited cry as she pulled out a NUKE ampule from the clumsy thief's pocket. She pressed it to her neck. Pfffftttt. In a matter of seconds, she was the envy of her peer group.

The gang of hookers marched down the street, leaving the moaning punk lying in his own spit on the cold Old Detroit macadam.

They strode down the avenue, passing an old-fashioned, broken-bottle donnybrook involving two drunken couples and a five-dollar bill.

They sauntered by a station wagon parked on a deserted street. The hookers let out a communal seductive moan at the young man behind the wheel, a punky-looking guy named Buzz. "Awww, fug-goff," he ordered. "I'm busy here."

"Pocket pool?" one girl catcalled, as they continued to undulate their way across Old Detroit.

"Hoooors," Buzz howled back. He glanced nervously across the street at a deserted gun store. As he watched, the building blew up.

Buzz flinched in the front seat as shards of glass and metal rained down upon his car. He revved up the engine. "About fuggin' time," he muttered. "You're absolute shit with a timer."

Buzz pulled the station wagon directly in front of the half-demolished store. He deftly made his way inside, avoiding the larger chunks of burning debris. "Fuggin' A!" he chuckled.

Inside the shattered shop, his three punk friends—Brad, Flint, and Chet—tumbled down the aisles toward him, their arms laden with pistols, shotguns, machine guns, ammo, and grenades. Chet, a hood who resembled a hard-core Beaver Cleaver, wielded his own particular favorite—a cache of Stinger missiles.

"Look at this!" he chortled. "I've joined the army!"

Buzz whirled around as a haunting moan filled the store. "What the hell . . ."

Behind the blasted-away counter, the bleeding form of the elderly store owner was sprawled. Buzz grinned evilly at the owner. "Well, whadda we got here?"

The owner raised a bloodied hand, in a sign of surrender. Buzz picked up an Auto-9 pistol and slapped in a cartridge. He gazed from the gun to the bleeding man. "Nasty-looking bullets," he said. "What are these, man?"

"Armor-piercing," the bleeding man offered meekly. Then he recognized the look on Buzz's face. "Oh, God . . ."

"I really like this gun," Buzz stated.

"Please. Take it and get out."

Buzz grinned at the moaning man. "Thanks, pop. I'll do just that."

He raised the pistol and fired a round into the man's face, reducing it to nothing more than crimson pudding and skull fragments.

"Great bullets," Buzz concluded. "Very effective."

He heard a noise behind him. He spun around, grinning, as a small army of street people began tumbling through the ruptured storefront, eager to snatch whatever they could.

"We've got company," Buzz said.

"Fuggin' thieves," Chet muttered sarcastically.

The four punks opened fire on the marauding street people, slicing half a dozen of them in two and sending the rest scattering.

"There's never a cop around when you really need one," said Buzz with a sigh. "Come on, let's go."

The four punks leaped out of the store and headed for their station wagon. The silence of the empty street was shattered by the wail of a siren.

"Huh?" uttered Buzz.

"Shit!" Chet hissed. "I don't believe this."

"It's the cops, man," Flint added.

"Cops are on strike, stupid," Chet pointed out.

"Can't you *hear* it?" asked Flint.

"It's an ambulance," Chet suggested. "*Got* to be . . ."

The four thugs froze, bathed in the angry glare of approaching headlights. They stood gaping, like possums caught in a bright light, at the police TurboCruiser speeding down the street toward them.

"Shit!" Chet swore, training a Stinger missile on the approaching auto. "This should slow the sucker down."

The other three boys cackled as Chet squeezed off a round from the shoulder-held, bazookalike weapon. The Stinger screamed down the street, smashing into the front of the cruiser. The car was promptly enveloped in a ball of flame, the impact from the missile sending it high into the air.

"Bull's-eye!" Buzz roared.

The cruiser bounced to the ground and continued, end over end, down the street. Bits of flaming metal fragments cascaded into the air. The cruiser finally smashed to a stop, and the scene was quiet.

"Let's have fun," Buzz suggested.

The four punks opened up on the remains of the auto, sending slug after slug of every type of weapon imaginable slicing into the sizzling wreckage.

From within the inferno, something stirred.

The four hoods lowered their guns and cocked their heads inquisitively. Nearly obscured by the smoke and fire, the driver's door of the cruiser swung open.

"I'm not seeing this," muttered Buzz.

"Me neither," said Chet.

A large metal-encased foot slammed down onto the fire-stained street. A large shadowshape emerged from the car. The four punks gaped at the helmeted figure emerging. It was a cop, but *more* than a cop. It was a being that resembled a cross between a knight of old and a high-tech football player. A sinewy, shining warrior of the new age.

"Oh, shit!" wailed Flint. "It's *HIM*, man! The Robodude!"

"Kill the fucker!" Buzz ordered.

The four punks raised their weapons and fired a fusillade of bullets at the advancing cyborg, their eyes wild with terror.

RoboCop continued his advance, slowly and surely. He lowered his right hand, his Auto-9 pistol slamming into his fist from a thigh holster, as bullets richocheted harmlessly off his metallic chest.

Robo scanned the area, activating his target grid. The four punks stood immobile before him. He quickly calculated the best trajectory and raised his pistol, squeezing off three quick shots. It wasn't a particularly challenging encounter.

Chet was the first to fall, spinning dizzily as his midsection tumbled down onto his knees.

Buzz found himself airborne, a gaping hole where his heart had been. Buzz's body slammed into the hood of the station wagon, sliding over it and down onto the sidewalk on the opposite side. His heart, however, landed where his feet had been seconds before, hitting the pavement with a resounding *squoosh*.

Brad stopped shooting abruptly as one of Robo's bullets entered the front of his forehead and his brains exited through a gaping hole in the rear of his head. Brad's body hit the ground like a sack of dung.

Robo faced the remaining thug, the shaking slimeball named Flint. "Peace officer," said Robo simply.

Flint dropped his weapon. "This is too much to handle, man!"

He reached into his pocket for a NUKE ampule. "I can't cope with this, man."

He began to raise the ampule to his neck. In a move of incredible grace and speed, Robo sprinted forward, grabbing the boy's wrist. Quickly holstering his gun, he snatched the ampule from the punk and crushed it in his hand.

He gazed at the crushed vial, analyzing it. Drug. Illegal. Chemically made. Neurotoxin.

He lifted the squirming thug named Flint high into the air. "Who makes this toxin?"

"I dunno!" the punk wailed.

Robo repeated the question, his voice nearly as steely as his presence. "Who . . . makes . . . *this*?"

"I don't *know*, man! All I know is where I get it."

RoboCop slowly lowered the trembling punk. "That is an excellent start," he said stiffly. "Now, you have the right to remain silent. . . ."

4

RoboCop's massive feet crunched through a small ocean of discarded NUKE ampules. With each step, he sent shards of the hard plastic vials shattering. He scanned the street, using his RoboVision. All seemed normal, if you could call a street such as this normal.

"NUKE Me!" and "NUKE Reigns!" slogans were spray-painted on walls with a fluorescent hue. Street people lay curled in the corner of every alleyway, shivering while sleeping, trying to evade the long tendrils of the dank, night air. The streets were filled with garbage and discarded, burnt-out cars. The storefronts were boarded up.

The place resembled an urban graveyard.

And that, Robo concluded, was exactly what it was.

Far behind him, beyond his sensory systems, a large Harley-Davidson was heading for the same neighborhood. The rider wore a helmet. Skulls and swastikas were painted all along the chopper. The rider calmly sent the hog off a freeway offramp.

It rumbled to a stop, its metallic kickstand sending up a small shower of sparks.

The helmeted figure removed a CompuMap from a jacket pocket and gazed at it. The rider knew where the chopper was. The rider knew where the chopper had to go.

In the streets ahead of the chopper, Robo still marched through the deserted streets and alleyways. He stopped before the remnants of an Italian restaurant, a small, humble, family affair, long closed down. Boarded up. Graffiti-laden. Robo swiveled his visored head this way and that, activating his thermograph. There was heat nearby.

He focused on the chimney of the "abandoned" building.

In Robo's eyes, the chimney glowed with a steady stream of pulsating heat.

Robo strode to the side of the restaurant, warily scanning the neighborhood. A silver stretch limo was parked in the shadow of the restaurant. Odd, Robo thought. Out of place. Expensive car, dead area.

Robo approached a side door to the restaurant. He carefully pried the boards free of the door, making sure that the creaking noises supplied by the rusted nails did not make too much of a racket.

He slowly swung the old door open. He tilted his head. From deep within the building, he could hear the sound of muffled music. RoboCop gently placed a heavy foot down upon the splintered floorboards of the place and, heightening his hearing senses, slowly followed the music to its source.

It was coming from what was once the kitchen of the restaurant.

Robo strained his hearing.

Inside the kitchen, there was something cooking. The odors and noises made from the equipment therein were clearly not the product of ordinary culinary utensils and pans.

Robo paused outside a large metal door that separated himself from the kitchen.

He knocked softly.

A small rectangular hatch opened, and a startled face filled three-quarters of the resulting hole. Robo quickly scanned the kitchen. Inside was a chemical-factory operation. Latin and Oriental women were feeding drops of the drug called NUKE from large canisters bearing the NUKE logo into small ampules. Others were placing the filled ampules into NUKE dispensers. One woman in the far corner tended to two babies. The atmosphere, as well as Robo could ascertain, was cheerful and relaxed, almost as if the kitchen were still being run as a family operation.

"Oh, shit!" the guard on the other side of the door moaned. "Not tonight."

Robo snapped to, sending his hand crashing through the door. He grabbed the guard by the throat and pulled him forward into the punctured portal. The guard's head slammed into the fractured door, and, dropping his weapon, the man collapsed onto the ground.

Remembering the countless ODed teenagers he had managed to scrape off the streets of Detroit,

Robo put his shoulder into the door and sent it tumbling inside.

The women workers panicked, screeching as they fled in every direction.

Half a dozen other guards began firing their AK-47s wildly. The women continued to scream, scrambling for cover.

Robo stood confused amid the pandemonium. Gaping at the terrified women, the first directive flashed across his field of vision: Serve the public trust.

He must protect the women.

He marched forward. A guard across the room opened fire, sending metal shards cascading down Robo's metallic side. Robo quickly pulled his pistol, shifted to target mode, and dropped the guard with a single shot. The guard flew through the air, smashing into the beakers and vials percolating in the room.

Robo whirled at the sound of movement. Switching to RoboVision, he gazed across the kitchen to a small window separating the sweatshop from an office in back. Robo focused. Beyond the small window, a small, sallow-faced boy picked up a tiny portable computer and slid it neatly into his slightly oversized jacket. The boy glanced across the office.

A spandex-clad, raven-haired woman snarled and quickly slammed a suitcase closed. Robo slipped his being into record mode, watching the diminutive boy and the Amazon head for a rear door. There they encountered a fierce-looking scarecrow of a man. The man looked like a well-dressed skeleton, a grizzled beard topping his pointed chin, a rakishly tilted top hat perched upon his head. He wore what appeared to be a custom-made yet ragtag tuxedo. This must be the leader, RoboCop concluded.

Robo examined the clothing of the threesome carefully. Very expensive. Terminally hip in a haphazard way. Out of place for a factory. Robo was still pondering the incongruity of it all when the trio disappeared from his view and the room around him erupted.

Two guards burst into the kitchen, firing Pancor assault shotguns.

Robo twirled his pistol, nailing one between the eyes.

A sudden roar.

Car engine, Robo concluded. No: too fierce. Motorcycle engine.

As Robo reached that conclusion, the chopper's driver leaped into the maelstrom, still wearing a dark helmet. Robo instinctively pulled back as the driver pulled the trigger of the gun. The bullet sent a second marauding guard sailing into a wall, leaving a scattershot trail of blood in his wake.

Another guard aimed a machine gun at the rider. The rider tumbled back out of the room, just a step ahead of a percolating wave of molten lead.

Robo spun around and downed the guard with a single bullet to the neck.

Outside the restaurant, the rider pulled off the dark helmet, revealing a close-cropped mane of auburn hair and a pair of lightly made-up lips. Officer Anne Lewis lifted up a handheld ComLink communicator.

"I found Murphy," she wheezed. "We've got ourselves a real situation here."

Inside the kitchen, meanwhile, Robo continued to diffuse the situation. One sniveling guard remained, and he had grabbed hold of two sobbing women. Chuckling softly, the guard held them both to his chest, effectively creating a human shield between himself and the square-jawed law-enforcement agent.

"You can't get me now, tin-can man," he jabbered. "I read the papers. I know what you can do and what you can't do. You're screwed now, you bag of bolts. Hey! I made a joke! Screwed? Bolts? Sometimes I kill myself."

"No," Robo said, gently, "*you* do not."

The guard stopped, puzzled.

Robo stared impassively at the scene, activating the grid on his RoboVision. Through his visor, he clicked into targeting mode. He tilted his head this way and that, attempting to conjure up a suitable path of fire that would eliminate the perpetrator while saving the lives of his two pleading hostages.

No matter how much he concentrated, his computerized sense of possible trajectory paths would not approve a final course of action. No matter where Robo aimed, the women would be in the way.

The guard began to sweat it, pointing a machine gun at the head of one of the sobbing women.

Robo blinked at the guard. His RoboVision flashed. Directive Two: Protect the innocent.

The guard began to chuckle. "Back off, tin man. You got it? *Back off!* You're going through that 'protect the innocent' crap, right? Ahahaha! I knew it."

The guard sent his head back with a roar of laughter. Robo glanced at the ceiling as well. In his RoboVision, the entire scene took on another angle. Robo suddenly saw the view from overhead. Adjusting his internal computers, a possible line of attack formed on the gridlines materializing before his eyes.

Robo smiled thinly. "Yes, you are right," he said. "I am defeated."

He caught a small glimmer of movement from the rear of the building. "Lewis!" he thundered. "Get down!"

Anne Lewis hit the ground immediately as Robo squeezed off a round from his powerful Auto-9 pistol. The tracer bullet smashed into a wall on the far side of the room and then spiraled into a second and a third, before careening into the guard's skull.

The man dropped like a stone, releasing the two screaming women.

Robo marched up to Lewis. "Are you all right?"

"Murphy," Lewis said, scrambling to her feet, "as your long-time partner, buddy, and welder, have I told you, lately, that you're a complete fool?"

RoboCop thought about this. "Not since yesterday at 9:15 A.M."

"Then you're due, fool," Lewis said, smiling.

"We have criminals to apprehend," RoboCop declared, facing the back alleyway. "Outside. Stretch limo. Felons."

"I get the picture," Lewis muttered, following Robo out of the restaurant.

Down the block, the raven-haired Amazon named Angie and the angular soul called Cain slid into the back seat of their limo. Their driver, Catzo, as big as an ox but not quite as smart, bit his lip.

"Where's Hob?" Catzo asked.

"That boy is incorrigible," Cain muttered.

Suddenly, the limo was assaulted by the sound of pounding fists. Cain lowered his window dapperly. A middle-aged woman crouched next to his door, sobbing for mercy. "Let me in! Please! Let me in!"

"It would really bother me." Cain sighed. "There are three people in here already, and we're hoping for a fourth."

"Really," Angie said, smiling sweetly. "He can't help himself. He's claustrophobic."

"It's true," said Cain to the distraught woman. "I'm really sorry."

Cain nodded at Catzo, motioning toward the woman. The gorilla of a chauffeur whipped a small pistol from his side and, aiming it at the startled woman, sent a shard of lead screaming into her skull. The woman tumbled back from the limo, stone-cold dead.

Hob, the young boy with the computer, scrambled out of a back doorway of the restaurant, nearly landing in a startled RoboCop's arms. The boy stood there, smiling. Robo froze. Behind him, Lewis was picking up speed. The elfin Hob pointed a silver-plated Automag at Robo, who quickly clicked into targeting mode. The target, trained on the boy's head, dissolved as soon as it was formed.

"Can't shoot a *kid*, can you, fucker?" Hob cackled.

Robo stood there stiffly.

"Murphy!" Lewis called from behind.

Hob squeezed off a harsh round. Robo, still frozen by the sight of a smiling child with a lethal weapon, took the blow in the head.

The bullet careened from his helmet, leaving a large scratch. Robo staggered, nearly collapsing to his knees.

"Murphy!" Lewis cried again.

Robo shook his head clear. Hob's recorded voice echoed in his ears like a long-playing record with a bad groove. "Can't shoot a kid, can you? Can't shoot a kid, can you? Can you? Can you? *Fucker!*"

Robo squinted into the darkness as Hob trotted to the awaiting limo. The boy leaped into the back, and the limo pulled away with a deafening screech.

Robo slowly straightened himself. "Felon," he whispered. "Child felon . . ."

"Nice going," Lewis said, hiding her concern for her partner. "I go to get myself some coffee. I'm gone *five*—"

"Fifteen," Robo corrected.

"*Fifteen* minutes," Lewis yelled, "and I have to spend the rest of the night trying to catch up with you!"

Anne Lewis gazed at Robo's creased skull-helmet, determined not to show her worry. "Then, of course, I have to go and commandeer a motorcycle. The bikers weren't very understanding. . . . They looked like living proof of anti-Darwinism."

Robo's entire body shuddered. He stiffened, withdrawing into himself. "You should not be here, Lewis."

"Yeah, yeah," she replied. "I know. This is off-limits to cops, like most of the city is."

He turned his back on her. She took a finger and ran it gently across the scratch in his helmet.

"Does that hurt, Murphy?" she asked timidly.

Robo shook his head from side to side. He was incapable of hurt now. He was incapable of . . .

Lewis withdrew her hand, puffing up her chest like a good cop. "Christ! That was just a kid that shot you! He couldn't have been more than—what? Ten? Eleven years old?"

"They . . . use . . . kids," Robo intoned softly. He felt saddened, both for discovering this fact and actually witnessing it. It wasn't sadness; that wasn't it. Sadness was an unknown factor. It was . . . an intellectual disappointment. The human race was devolving. *That*'s what made him feel so sa—disappointed.

Lewis turned away from RoboCop's turmoil. "Those bastards are *smart*," she said. "We can't shoot minors. Can't even keep them locked up. Most we can do is send them to juve hall. Hell, that's a walk in the park for *them*. They're in and out of there in a few hours and . . . Whoah! Look at this, Murphy!"

Anne Lewis stooped over in the alley, Robo standing, dazed, above her. She picked up what looked like a candy bar. It was studded with tiny NUKE ampules.

"Just look at this, will ya! NUKE . . . packaged like candy so that it can be sold to kids in schoolyards. For lunch money. The bastards!"

Not saying a word, RoboCop turned on his heels

and marched down the street, leaving a startled Officer Anne Lewis in his wake.

"Hey, Murphy?" she called.

Robo continued to march forward into the dark, dank night.

"Murphy?" Lewis repeated. "RoboCop? Robo? Partner?"

Robo continued his march.

"Goddamnit, Murphy," Lewis said, trotting after him. "Don't go doing anything stupid. Don't you dare go shutting me out again. Talk to me, Murphy! Goddamn you! Talk to me!"

Robo disappeared into the swirls of mist and grit just as a TurboCruiser pulled up. An officer named Dante stuck his head out of the car. "Any trouble?"

"Our trouble's over for tonight," Lewis said.

"Where's your partner?" Dante asked.

"That's tomorrow's trouble."

5

The first blotches of the morning sun that fought their way through the clouds over the city bathed the Old Detroit stationhouse in a mottled, orange glow. The building looked more like the Alamo than a precinct house. Bullet holes pockmarked the outside of the ancient brick building. Most of the police TurboCruisers parked in the street outside boasted a myriad of dents and scratches.

Although it was only first light, a group of sullen police officers carrying picket signs had already gathered.

RoboCop guided a cruiser toward the underground parking-garage entrance, easing it carefully through the picketing cops. Shouts of "Scab!" greeted his arrival. Lewis sat silently at his side.

A cop on the picket line trotted up to Lewis's open window. The cop offered her a sneer, nodding toward RoboCop. "Him, I could believe it of, Lewis. He has no *choice*. But I never figured *you* for a goddamned *scab*."

Lewis returned the sneer. "And I figured you for a cop, Stef. I guess we're both wrong."

Robo accelerated slightly, sending the car rumbling down the driveway. The cop named Stef shook an angry fist at the retreating vehicle.

"The union's got a list, Lewis," he shouted. "We ain't forgetting who you are!"

"I hate that man," Lewis muttered.

"His use of slang doesn't enhance the department's image," Robo conceded.

Inside the stationhouse, the booking desk reflected the chaos engulfing the city. Civilian volunteers tried to man the phones. A holding tank was loaded to the brim with lowlifes who were all, to a man, "innocent," the victims of a bum rap. In the background, a deranged woman screamed a mantra of insanity.

Lewis and Robo entered the room. Wounded cops staggered in and out of doorways.

Lewis sighed and removed her flak jacket. "Home, sweet home." She sighed, turning to Robo. "Gotta shower. I'll catch up with you."

Robo nodded. "Thanks for the loan of the car."

"What are partners for?" She smiled, entering the overcrowded locker room.

If the outside of the station resembled the exterior of the Alamo, then the locker room surely reflected the inside of that historical house of carnage. Since the strike had begun, the few cops who did show up for work were pulling more than their share of shifts. They were outnumbered and outgunned on the streets, their presence providing little more than a bandage for the gaping wound known as Detroit.

Lewis slowly undid her blouse, watching exhausted cops of both sexes bandage themselves before staggering into the showers. She unslung her gunbelt and hung it on her locker door.

A frazzled sergeant named Reed led a stunned and bloodied cop by her. Reed caught the eye of a nurse across the room. "Call an ambulance, god-damnit!" he bellowed. "We sure as hell can't help him here!"

Reed softened his features, propping up the dazed rookie.

"You'll be okay, Mesnik."

He glanced at a cheerful rotund cop who was in the process of sliding on a flak jacket. Reed checked his watch. "That's two shifts tonight, Duffy," he said. "You're pushing it too hard."

The other cop shrugged. "Tough times need tough cops, Sergeant. I'm fine."

Duffy loaded his pistol, whistling softly, then holstered it and marched out of the room. Lewis eyed him suspiciously, nodding toward Reed. "Never seen Duffy so eager, Sarge."

Reed nodded. "Robo come back with you, Lewis?"

"Yeah. He's in records. Cross-referencing his memory with the mug file."

"Christ!" Reed muttered. "Keep an eye on him, will ya? The last thing I need is him getting pulverized battling twenty hopheads at a time."

"Will do," Lewis promised.

Downstairs in CompuLab, Robo strode silently past the rows of computer banks and monitors, forcing the kibitzing data processors to lapse into silence. Even after all this time, they still weren't used to seeing the metallic mountain of a cop prowl about the station.

Robo marched to a point before a massive computer. Extending his right hand, he flipped out his built-in, metal-accessing strip—a frightening appendage that resembled a stiletto. Robo inserted the strip into the computer's access port. The video monitor before him snapped to life as Robo downloaded his recorded scenes from earlier in the morning.

The faces of Cain and Angie appeared in the sweatshop office. Robo zoomed in on their faces and held the scene. He then called up a series of mug shots on the right hand of the video terminal. He fast-forwarded through thousands of them, attempting to match eyes, mouth, noses, and shapes of heads.

"SUBJECTS NOT FOUND," announced the computer.

Puzzled, Robo downloaded the furious face of elfin Hob, raising the gun toward RoboCop's face.

Robo twisted his fist and called up the avalanche of mug shots once more. First the eyes appeared. Then the mouth. Finally, the nose and the entire face.

He had a match.

"HOB MILLS: AGED TWELVE. LAST SEEN: HAMTRAMCK GROUND ZERO VIDEO ARCADE."

A data processor wearing hoot-owl glasses sidled up behind Robo. He stared at the screen as Robo twisted his extended hand again, attempting to call up Hob's rap sheet.

"ACCESS DENIED," the computer declared.

"I bet the little bastard's lawyer had his record sealed," the data processor muttered. "The little turd is probably a hit man."

Robo silently withdrew his accessing strip, reinserted the spike in his hand, and, without saying a word, left the CompuLab. "Remember when kids were just kids?" the processor called after Robo's retreating form.

Robo marched back into the main room of the precinct, passing by a cell block filled with young criminals and NUKE addicts. Over a dozen young offenders were crammed into a cell made for six.

"Hey, here comes RoboFag!" yelled one.

"Eat shit, bullethead!" called another.

"Hey, RoboShit," another one yelped, "screw any cruisers lately?"

Robo spun around and faced the young perps, a strange look on his face. The felons settled down immediately, staring up at the icy-blue eyes beneath the clear visor. They were clearly frightened, and, for a split second, Robo saw them for what they truly were: kids.

He marched past the locker room. Pausing at the door, he stared inside. There, rinsing the lather from her body, was Anne Lewis. Robo regarded her naked body in silence. Lewis turned, startled, and met RoboCop's gaze. He stood frozen in the doorway for a moment, before turning and marching down the hall, without uttering a sound. Confused and concerned, Lewis scrambled out of the shower and quickly donned a fresh uniform.

She bolted out of the locker room and ran down to

the small RoboChamber, the computer-laden cubicle Robo called home. His massive form was missing from the large chair hooked up to his monitoring devices.

Lewis glanced around nervously. Robo's head technician, Tak Akita, was in the midst of a screaming session on a telephone. His partner, Linda Garcia, fiddled with a computer console impatiently.

"This sucks," she hissed.

"Don't make our job *impossible*!" Tak shouted into the receiver. "We're losing hours with this program! It's an antique! You hired us to maintain and study Robo! No! I will not hold. I've been holding for the last twenty-five—hello? *Hello?*"

He slammed the phone down. "Shit!" He turned to Garcia. "No go. We'll have to make do with the old program."

"It'll take days to collate the new data," Garcia said glumly.

Lewis offered a tentative wave of her hand. "Problems?"

"The usual crap from OCP." Tak sighed, turning to his consoles. "They treat Robo like he's yesterday's news. Won't spend a dime to update his software."

Lewis glanced at Robo's empty chair. "How's he doing? He doesn't seem to be himself lately."

"I could write a short thesis on his REM patterns if I had the software," Tak answered.

"REM patterns?" Lewis asked.

"Rapid eye movement. Happens during the dream phase of sleep," Tak answered.

"I still don't get it."

"Our boy's been dreaming like a sonofabitch," Tak replied. "Want to see?"

He pressed a key on a computer keyboard lying before a video terminal. The video screen zapped to life. A myriad of images flashed in and out of one another, forming a sort of cerebral collage.

A football glided high into the air, caught by a pair of hands directly in front of the video screen.

The next screen image was the back seat of a car and a furious necking session with a cheerleader.

A nun screamed at the viewers, waving a yardstick in her hand.

Snow clung to a tree in the middle of a harsh winter.

A rolling thunderhead cascaded across an azure-blue sky.

A murderer named Clarence Boddiker raised his shotgun and blew a blast of molten lead directly at the screen.

"What is all this?" Lewis asked, suppressing a shiver.

"Murphy's life," Tak explained. "He's done an amazing job of reconstructing his human memory. We're seeing fragments of it here from his point of view."

"Amazing," Lewis said.

Tak nodded in agreement, pressing another key.

"Lately, though, he's been fixing in on three key subjects."

On the screen before them, a young woman dried herself in a bathroom following a shower. She was naked, and she seemed to shoo the camera away, making a funny face at it.

"His wife, Ellen," Tak said.

Hands appeared on the screen, tossing a baby into the air.

"His son, Jimmy," Tak added.

A helmeted cop took a swing at a felon, neatly cold-cocking the perp. The cop removed her helmet. Anne Lewis's smiling face winked at the screen.

Lewis's form was replaced by that of Ellen Murphy, writhing in bed as an unseen Murphy made love to her.

"His wife, his kid . . . and you," Tak whispered.

Lewis felt her face redden. "Shut that off, will you?"

Tak did as he was told. Lewis's lips began to tremble. "God, he's really *hurting*."

"Not likely," Tak replied, matter-of-factly. "They were pretty selective about what sectors of his brain they utilized during the reconstructive surgery. His emotional range is virtually nonexistent."

"Then why is he dredging up his memories at all?" Lewis asked.

"I dunno." Tak shrugged. "Maybe he's just curious."

Lewis glared at the scientist. "You're wrong,"

she said firmly. "He's more of a man than you know."

Lewis turned and strode out of the room, leaving a puzzled Tak and Garcia behind.

"What's the matter with her?" Tak asked.

"She's a cop," said Garcia. "What more do you have to know?"

6

RoboCop guided his TurboCruiser through the well-kept Detroit suburb. He glanced at the shrubbery. Nicely trimmed. Flowers bloomed. How far this all seemed from the hellishness of Old Detroit.

He scanned the streets, purposefully. A young boy, no more than twelve years of age, darted from his home and ran up to a mailbox. The mailbox bore the name "Murphy."

RoboCop slowed the car.

The young boy looked up.

Something within Robo churned painfully. The boy, his face beaming, gazed into the car.

Robo tried to avoid the young boy's stare. He gunned the gas, sending the cruiser accelerating down the street. The twelve-year-old named Jimmy turned and sprinted toward the house, stumbling over his bicycle as he ran.

"Mom!" he shouted. "Mom! Get my camera!"

Ellen Murphy emerged from the nicely painted home, alarmed. "What? What is it?"

Seeing his mother's concerned face, Jimmy

sighed and ran past her. "Never mind. I'll get it myself."

"What happened, Jimmy?" his mother asked.

Jimmy trotted out of the house, screwing the lens onto his camera. "RoboCop!" he said, charging toward his bicycle. "He was right here! Right outside our house! I saw him!"

Jimmy leaped onto his bike and pedaled furiously down the street, attempting to catch up with the TurboCruiser. Ellen watched him go.

She stared down the empty street, her face ashen. Her body suddenly unsteady, she braced against the doorway for support. It didn't offer the type she needed.

Miles away from the suburban tract, a lone police TurboCruiser charged back in the direction of the Detroit skyline.

Its driver, his metallic hands clutching the wheel, tried to put as much distance as possible between the suburb and himself. He pressed down on the accelerator.

It would never be enough distance.

Never enough.

7

Something was abuzz at OCP. Rumors concerning the robotics R&D team were circulating up and down the halls like wildfire. At this point no one could say whether something wonderful or something dreadful was going on down at research and development, but everyone was excited nonetheless. Where rumors went, the Old Man followed. And it had been some time since the Old Man blew a gasket. It was really something to see.

Dr. Juliette Faxx was impressed by neither rumors nor the prospect of seeing someone develop heartburn. She had her own agenda. She walked coolly down the hall, her long dark hair cascading over her shoulders. With ice-white skin and dark brown eyes, Faxx had the kind of looks men would die for. In fact, some OCP wags insisted that that was indeed the case.

Faxx took it all in stride. Women were always jealous of beauty, and men always disdained that which they could not possess.

Faxx strolled down one of OCP's massive product-display hallways, her young assistant, Jenny, falling into step behind her.

"Good morning, Jenny," Faxx said. "What have we got this morning?"

Jenny consulted her notepad. "General Gonzaga canceled: Apparently there's been a coup. But there's a gentleman from the private sector interested in defense robotics."

Faxx shrugged, entering a large pristine showroom displaying models of all of OCP's robotic triumphs, past and present. A tall angular man sporting a cocked top hat and a raven-haired woman dressed like a pop star stared at the displays. Faxx frowned. Great. This is just what she needed today: two eccentrics.

Jenny handed Faxx a readout. "Here's his credit sheet."

Faxx smiled in approval at the man's credit forms. The man named Cain had money to burn. "He's certainly financially qualified," she acknowledged. "I'll handle it from here."

"Yes, Dr. Faxx," Jenny replied, slowing her pace.

Faxx walked briskly into the room, affixing a salesperson's smile on her face.

Cain and Angie had been walking by a display showing a full-sized model of the ED209 robots and had paused before a full-sized RoboCop statue. Angie nudged Cain. The angular man turned and greeted Faxx with a wide, friendly smile.

"Good day, Mr. Cain," Faxx said.

Cain executed a slight bow. "Doctor. You look lovely today."

Angie wasn't as impressed. "Love the blouse."

Faxx was startled. "I'm sorry. Have we met before?"

Angie produced a high-tech Filofax from her studded black-leather purse. "Juliette Faxx, Ph.D., psychology, graduate *summe cum laude* Harvard University, three years' private practice, now director of marketing, Security Concepts, OCP."

Faxx cocked her head inquisitively. "Is there something I can help you with?"

Angie nodded toward the Robo statue. "Yeah. He'll take one of those."

Faxx laughed softly. "I'm afraid we're unable to accommodate you."

"Hey!" Angie frowned. "His money's good."

"I'm sure it is," Faxx conceded, "but even if we had one to offer, it wouldn't be available to private accounts."

Angie shot Faxx a blistering look before leaning toward Cain. "Guess you have to own a country to get a RoboCop, honey."

Cain was not dissuaded. "Get somebody on it. Somebody with an accent."

Angie typed a note in her Filofax, while Cain grinned slyly in Faxx's direction. "You don't have to own a country to fight a war, dear doctor."

"OCP is committed to peace, not war," Faxx pointed out dutifully. "Maintaining the peace."

Cain emitted a good-natured chuckle. "Maintaining the status quo, you mean. Keeping the people down. And you used to be a psychologist. A *healer*."

He turned to Angie. "You see, Angie? It's like I said: All it takes is money."

Faxx glared at Cain and the two made eye contact, Faxx barely suppressing her rage. Turning her back on the jaunty man, she gestured at small prototypes of robotic weaponry. "We do offer the private sector an impressive line of robot security systems. The auto-gatling series, for instance . . ."

Cain remained in place in front of the RoboCop statue. "Why'd you only make one RoboCop?" he asked.

"I'm not sure I know what you're—" Faxx began.

"I mean," Cain said, pointing to the statue, "all you need is a brain. The world is full of brains!"

Faxx tried to hide her discomfort. "What? Whatever are you talking about?"

"Brains," Cain said, pointing a finger at his own head in exasperation. "The only way to make smart robots. So you waited until a cop, um . . ."

He snapped his fingers, and Angie consulted her files. "Murphy," she replied. "Alex J., gunned down in the line of duty."

Cain flashed a smug smile. "See? You used his brain. Popped it right into that classy chassis."

Faxx was totally dumbfounded. The cybernetic techniques used in the construction of the RoboCop prototype were classified information. Angie seemed to read the doctor's mind. "It's all in your computers." Angie shrugged. "No big secret."

"Are you saying that you *accessed* our databanks?" Faxx snorted.

Cain raised and lowered his gangly arms innocently. "Not me, no. I have people who do that for me."

Cain leaned toward the RoboCop statue, scrutinizing a small printed legend concerning the prototype. "Angie?" he asked. "What does this say?"

Cain lowered his torso so Angie could softly read the printed words into his ear. Cain nodded, then faced the doctor. "See? I have people who read for me, too."

"You seem to have people who do almost everything," said Faxx coolly.

"Not *almost*." Cain grinned.

Angie consulted her files, still checking out the Robo model. "Nothing here that we don't know already," she announced.

"Except one small point." Cain nodded.

Angie motioned with her head toward Faxx. "You'll have to ask her."

Cain turned to Dr. Faxx. "How long is he going to be alive?"

"Interesting question," Faxx admitted. "All his parts are, of course, replaceable."

"So," Cain concluded, "if nobody destroys his brain, he might live forever. Touch the eternal."

Faxx pondered this. "We trust the unit will be functional . . . for a very long time to come."

The conversation drew to an abrupt halt when a beeping noise emerged from Faxx's coat pocket. Reaching inside, she produced a pocket pager and brought it to her ear. Her face tightened. "Yes, sir," she said into the two-way transmitter-receiver. "I'll be right along."

She turned on her heels and walked away, calling

to Cain over her shoulder. "My apologies, Mr. Cain. I have to go. Jenny will be in shortly to help you with anything the young lady can't read for you."

Cain watched her go, grinning like a maniac. The woman obviously liked her toys. Cain liked toys, too. He thought they had a lot in common.

8

The Old Man marched furiously down one of the glistening corridors at OCP headquarters. Behind him, a grim-faced Johnson and a sweating roboticist named Schenck struggled to keep up with him. Dr. Faxx emerged silently from an elevator and joined the small parade. Things were not looking good. Schenck, his left arm in a sling, was gesturing wildly with his right hand.

"Sir," he whined, "once again, I must emphasize that this project still has a way to go before we'll be ready."

"Five months, Mr. Schenck," the Old Man intoned in a low, powerful voice, "and ninety million dollars. I would like to see what you've got to show me!"

Schenck nodded like a marionette with cheap strings. "We *have* isolated the problem. It's not the *technology*. It's the *candidates*."

"What the devil are you talking about?" the Old Man barked back, his lips twitching.

"I believe I can show you, sir," Schenck wheezed. "If you'll step this way . . ."

Schenck eased open a door leading to an OCP robotics lab. The Old Man stepped inside.

Johnson and Faxx entered the room as well, following Schenck to a video monitor. Schenck popped a tape into the video system.

"What the hell is this?" the Old Man demanded. "A tape? Ninety million dollars for a tape?"

"It'll explain itself, sir," Schenck offered lamely. The Old Man, Faxx, and Johnson stared at the screen as a videotaped Schenck gestured proudly at a pair of titanic metal doors. The doors swung open and a gleaming, sleek cyborg entered the room. A technician attempted to shadow its every move, still working on the cyborg's chest with a small welder.

Another technician adjusted the cyborg's blank, mannequinlike face. A flurry of electrical pulses slowly brought the face to life, giving it distinct features and a personality of sorts.

"State-of-the-art destructive capability commanded by a unique combination of organic and software systems," the videotaped Schenck announced. "In every way an improvement over the original."

The cyborg's still-forming face emitted a silent scream, its features contorting in a mask of pain and shock.

"Ladies and gentlemen," the on-screen Schenck cooed grandly, "it gives me great pleasure to introduce RoboCop 2!"

The cyborg shuddered and, pushing the technician away from its chest, grabbed the welding tool and turned the ice-blue flame on its face. Sparks burst forth from its skull. The two technicians scrambled to safety as the cyborg's head exploded in a sudden eruption of flesh and microchips.

The Old Man sat in stoney silence. Schenck fast-forwarded the tape to yet another unveiling.

A second cyborg stood behind a videotaped Schenck. ". . . the future of urban pacification. Ladies. Gentlemen. RoboCop 2!"

This time, the fully finished cyborg gazed vacantly around the room. Its eyes fell upon a shiny slab of metal. It bent over to gaze at its own reflection. Recoiling in horror, the cyborg let out a heart-wrenching shriek and, raising its metallic hands, ripped its own head off.

Schenck fast-forwarded the tape again.

The Old Man's eyes had narrowed themselves to slits now. He was seething.

On the screen, a third cyborg materialized. A videotaped Schenck was in the middle of his spiel when the cyborg glanced down at its stiff, Olympian body.

". . . proud to present . . ." intoned the video Schenck.

The cyborg, traumatized by its metallic self, drew its pistol with a roar.

"Hey!" Schenck squealed on screen. "Hold on, guy!"

The cyborg sent a shot slamming into Schenck's arm, sending the robotics expert twirling over a computer console. The others in the room hit the floor as the cyborg began firing his pistol randomly. Finally, satisfied with the commotion it had caused, the cyborg raised the gun to its head and blew its brains out.

Schenck turned the video machine off. The four sat in silence, a small smile on Faxx's face. Schenck was covered with enough sweat to qualify him for irrigation. The Old Man glared at him. "I'm listening, Mr. Schenck."

"W-we've tried everything," Schenck stammered. "But there just seems . . . well, there's an emotional quotient that we just can't control."

The Old Man was aghast. "Robots with emotional problems?"

"Not robots . . . sir," Schenck corrected. "Cyborgs. Cybernetic organisms. We use living human tissue, and, frankly, that's our whole problem. It's not the hardware. We've tried to isolate the glitch—use only the parts of the brain that control motor functions—but each time we try . . . we . . . well, you saw."

"The candidates were all fine men," the Old Man declared. "Respected police officers. I reviewed their files myself. I can't see how—"

"If I may suggest something, sir?" Faxx injected.

"Certainly, ah, Dr. . . . ah . . ."

"Police officers might not be the best candidates for our purposes," Faxx concluded.

The Old Man clearly didn't understand. Faxx leaned flirtatiously closer to the despot, allowing him to smell the perfume on her hair. "Police officers are generally . . . macho," she continued. "Body-proud. Sexually active. It's not hard to imagine that, finding themselves stripped of all that, they become suicidal."

Johnson frowned. "But we take all that away from them. We don't use the parts of their brains that give them personality."

Faxx shrugged. "Something obviously survives. Look at Murphy. He managed to reclaim not only his human memory but an unmistakable sense of personal identity."

"Then why hasn't RoboCop killed himself?" Johnson asked.

"Ah," said Faxx, smiling and crossing her curvacious legs, "but he will. All the signs are there. Look at the unnecessary risks he takes. That's hardly in his program."

Johnson didn't seem pleased by the direction in which the conversation was heading. "With all due respect, Doctor Faxx, your area of expertise is marketing, and what we've seen is clearly not yet ready to be sold. I think we should defer to the experts."

Faxx shrugged. "Perhaps you're right. I wouldn't presume to be an expert in robotics. I'm only suggesting that, as Mr. Schenck explained, hardware is not your problem. It is the human factor."

The Old Man smiled at the woman. "Whatever your ideas are, I'm most interested in hearing them."

Johnson rolled his eyes as Faxx continued. "If a new subject could be found—someone to whom the prospect might even be desirable . . ."

"But how would we find people like that?" the Old Man queried.

"It would require a screening test," Faxx admitted. "But there are people such as I've described around. In fact, I've met a few of them."

"I've never met anyone who wanted to be a robot," Johnson grumbled.

"Cyborg," Schenck corrected.

"Shut up, Mr. Schenck," the Old Man said.

"I have," Schenck replied.

Faxx gestured at the array of robotic parts stored in the room. "It seems a shame to waste all this fine expensive work, doesn't it? Surely the cost of screening a few new candidates would be negligible. I can't help but think it might prove to be very worthwhile for OCP."

The Old Man nodded and got to his feet. "Of course it would be worthwhile! Begin at once!"

He walked toward the exit, a bounce in his step. He turned and waved at Dr. Faxx. "And report to me directly."

Faxx smiled and waved her hand. "Thank you, sir."

Johnson followed the Old Man out of the room in silence. Something had just gone down with the Old Man that Johnson didn't like. It smelled bad. For the first time in a long time, Johnson was afraid. He had seen what robotic experiments could do if not handled correctly. The result was always the same: bloodshed.

Maybe that was the odor he smelled.

PART TWO

"One should forgive one's enemies, but not before they are hanged."
— Heinrich Heine

9

Anne Lewis sat sipping coffee in a ragtag doughnut shop. Above her, the stars of early evening slogged their way through a low-hanging cloud cover.

Her body positioned on a seat facing the front window, Lewis watched the Ground Zero Video Arcade across the street.

She smiled to herself as the elfin figure of Hob ambled into the sparkling joint. She picked up a handheld Com device. "Your information was good, Murphy. The little darling just went inside."

She returned the ComLink device to her pocket and continued to watch the arcade entrance. Then her jaw dropped. Detroit Police Officer Ambrose Duffy, in full uniform, walked casually through the front door. Lewis clutched the miniComLink. "We've got problems, Murphy. It's Duffy. He just went inside. Yeah, *Duffy*. Officer Duffy! I don't know what the hell he's doing in there."

She pocketed the miniCom, slammed a bill down on the table, and slowly proceeded toward the arcade entrance.

Inside the arcade, it was a typical weekday night. The block-long building was brimming with kids with money to spend. Row upon row of video games illuminated the place with an eerie, spasmodic display of colors. Bloops, beeps, and blatts echoed off the walls.

Children of every age attacked the machines like sharks in a feeding frenzy—when they weren't pigging out on the latest of junk foods.

Through this electronic orgy waddled Officer Duffy. A sixteen-year-old girl wearing a skintight "NUKE ME" T-shirt sauntered up to him.

"One of these days, will you give me a break, Officer?" She smiled. Her eyes were dull and drugged.

Duffy smiled in return and moved on. He spotted the diminutive Hob attacking a large video game, surrounded by adoring peers. Duffy laid a pudgy hand on the back of the boy's shirt.

"Time to do time, twerp," he announced. Hob remained silent as Duffy collared him and led him toward the rear of the arcade. Kids began to stare.

Hob started yelling. "I'm *clean*, man! I'm *clean*!"

One of Hob's arcade cronies, a gargoyle of a kid named Munson, eased himself away from a video game and silently followed the pair toward the rear of the building.

Duffy dragged Hob to a back alley and tossed him onto the ground. Munson emerged, unheard, from the building. The gargoyle-boy said nothing. He simply closed the door behind him and watched.

Hob made sure no one else was around before he got to his feet, brushing dust off his expensive pants. "Okay, Duffy! Jesus! Enough with the reality, okay? You got my clothes dirty and everything."

"Come on," Duffy said, his body relaxing. "Set me up."

Hob smirked at Munson. "Oh, look who's hurting."

Duffy ignored Munson. "Come on! I'm due back at the station."

Munson and Hob exchanged glances. The latter nodded. Munson produced a gold-plated NUKE dispenser. Duffy's eyes gazed upon the glistening treat adoringly.

"The station . . ." Hob smiled, stalling. "How *are* things back there? Anything I ought to know about?"

"Plenty." Duffy nodded, nearly salivating. "They're canceling patrols from Hamtramck to Highland Park. Just giving up on those sectors. You want to move in? It'll be wide open."

The officer continued to stare at the drug dispenser. "Come on . . ."

Hob grinned. "What the hell. We're buddies, right?"

"Right!" Duffy nodded again, his face beginning to twitch. Munson handed the NUKE dispenser to him. Duffy opened the dispenser clumsily, his fat fingers fumbling with the latch. He removed an ampule and raised it to his neck.

Suddenly he found himself blinded by the fierce white light emitted from a TurboCruiser parked down the alleyway.

Duffy couldn't see the driver, but he heard a car

door swing open and a mighty, metallic foot slam into the macadam with a crash.

"Oh, shit!" exclaimed Duffy.

The two boys stood frozen as the massive frame of RoboCop stepped between them and the car lights, his public-address mode working perfectly. "Nobody move," Robo's voice thundered. "You are under arrest."

Caught in the unyielding glare of the headlights, the trio split up. Hob and Munson darted back into the video arcade while Officer Duffy turned tail and jogged down the alleyway in the opposite direction. RoboCop stared at the arcade, knowing full well that his partner was inside to tackle the two fleeing juveniles.

Robo marched down the alley after Duffy, who had come wheezing to a halt in front of one of the alleyway walls. Glancing about nervously, Duffy spotted a metal ladder and quickly began climbing, his pudgy hands scraping against the wall's brick surface. He heard the clanging of metallic footsteps echoing down the passageway below him.

Although he was a large man, Duffy skittered up the ladder with the speed of a prodded monkey. The roof of the building was soon in sight, and Duffy breathed a sigh of relief.

He extended his hand to the rooftop.

He felt the ladder lurch.

He gaped at the scene below him. RoboCop extended a hand and, grabbing the base of the ladder, gave an Olympian yank, tearing the base of the ladder out of its brick moorings.

Still using but one glistening hand, Robo jerked

the ladder downward, effectively sending all of the metal stairway's bolts zinging out of the wall. Above, Duffy found the ladder being sucked down out of his grip. He tumbled off the rusting bars and flew helplessly through space, his rotund body hurtling into a pile of garbage stacked haphazardly on the ground. Robo sent the bottom of the ladder crashing down through a reed-thin metallic street grate.

"Give me a break!" Duffy moaned, trying futilely to find his discarded ampule. "Man, I can't help myself. I'm hooked, Robo, I'm hooked!"

Duffy was yanked to his feet by his collar.

He gazed into the square-jawed visage of Robo-Cop, trying to ascertain what the cyborg's expression was telling him. Duffy gulped. It wasn't "have a nice day."

Inside the arcade, meanwhile, a nervous Munson and Hob shoved their way through the young crowd, heading for the front door. Lights blinked hellishly all around them, and the heavy-metal music being piped through the arcade's monolithic speakers was deafening. Hob was the first to come skidding to a stop, causing Munson to slam into his back. "Hey," Munson exclaimed, "what the heck do you—"

Before them, blocking their exit, was Officer Anne Lewis, her pistol aimed in a crouched, combat stance.

Hob and Munson exchanged furtive looks.

Hob lowered his hand to his side ominously. Lewis glanced about the crowd. "Out of the way!" she yelled at the kids, but the music completely drowned her out. Frustrated, Lewis attempted to find her way clear to a clean shot.

The sixteen-year-old "NUKE ME" girl wandered into her sights.

"Damnit!" Lewis yelled. "I said, *move it!*"

The girl remained in place, her glassy eyes focused on Lewis. "Oh, wow!" she whispered. "A lady cop!"

Lewis charged forward, shoving the girl out of the way. She stared into the crowd. Hob and Munson were gone.

The arcade crowd surged forward, catching Lewis in the flow. Sheathing her pistol, she found herself buffeted about.

Two rows away, Hob hopped behind a video display.

Lewis continued to fight the crowd, trying to recognize Hob and Munson in the sea of glassy-eyed faces. She twisted her way forward.

She saw one young boy's eyes widen suddenly, staring at a point behind her.

Lewis whirled as Munson leaped out of an arcade game at her back, his switchblade drawn. With no time to draw her weapon, Lewis extended her right hand forward and, wrapping it around the boy's extended arms, grabbed it and gave it a firm twist. The knife went clattering to the ground.

Seething now, Lewis took the boy's arm and wrapped it around his back, shoving him forward toward an arcade game. Howling profanities, the boy was sent tumbling face-first into an arcade screen, his face smacking into the display.

"Tilt," Lewis said.

She heard a feral growl from behind. Before she could pivot, Hob's elfin body had appeared atop a video game to her rear and launched itself at her.

Hob landed directly on Lewis's back, expertly wrapping his legs around her torso in a scissorhold. Producing a garrote from his pocket, he crossed the wire-thin rope around her neck and began to tighten it.

Munson, still in her grasp, began to squirm as Lewis tore frantically at the garrote with her free hand.

Lewis angrily shoved Munson forward, and his face shattered the video screen. From inside the unit, Munson began to cry.

Lewis raised both hands to the garrote. No use: It was too thin, already imbedded too deeply in her neck.

Summoning up all her strength, she began to backpedal furiously across the room, Hob still on her back and cackling like a monkey as he twisted and turned the garrote.

Lewis rammed backward into a large metal arcade game, Hob taking the brunt of the blow. The punk's pixielike features registered a state of total shock as he felt the wind being knocked from his body. His head pitched sideways, smacking into a sharp corner of the game.

Hob emitted a shocked cry, the yelp of a young child in the midst of a bad fall.

He released his grip on the garrote, instinctively reaching for his head. Hob toppled backward, coming to a rolling halt on the floor next to Lewis's feet. He was out cold.

Officer Lewis fought off dizziness. She dropped to her knees, gasping for breath.

She heard a screech.

She glanced up, trying to regain her vision, as Munson yanked his bleeding face out of the shattered video terminal in front of her.

The gargoyle-child began to laugh like some sort of wounded animal as he picked up his switchblade and approached Lewis. The officer attempted to shake her head clear. Her hands were trembling too much for her to pick up her gun.

Munson was whining nasally as he tossed the knife from one hand to another, a vicious grin on his face.

The boy suddenly discovered that his feet were no longer on the ground.

"Wothafug!" he exclaimed as an oversized hand slammed into the back of his neck and lifted him high into the air, as if he were made of paper.

"Lemme down! Lemme down!" Munson demanded in a high-pitched wheeze.

"As you wish," RoboCop said.

He flicked the boy high into the air. Munson sailed across the width of the arcade, smashing into a buzzing and undulating wall-sized light display.

An avalanche of brightly colored sparks sizzled out of the wall and across the arcade as Munson sliced across the neon and the wiring. His body writhed as the electrical shocks made their way through his nervous system. Before he hit the ground, the boy had lapsed into unconsciousness.

The lights in the arcade fluttered. Within seconds, the entire hall was plunged into darkness and silence.

The sixteen-year-old tart in the "NUKE ME" T-shirt surveyed the scene. "Wow!" she concluded. "*Maximum* thrash!"

Robo bent over his partner. "Are you all right?"

Lewis nodded, allowing herself to be helped to her feet. She massaged her neck with her left hand. "Yes," she whispered. "I may never sing opera again, though."

RoboCop nodded. "A great loss," he deadpanned.

Lewis shook her head in Robo's direction. "I've always loved your sense of humor, Murphy."

She nodded toward the two unconscious punks lying in the debris. "Come on," she said. "It's time to pick up the trash."

She walked to Hob. "And *this* is just one small mound of the junk pile."

Robo stared at Hob. "I know," he said evenly. "I know."

Anne Lewis shot a nervous glance in Robo's direction. She didn't like it when he readily agreed with her. It made her nervous. And usually with good reason.

10

The night shift was fending off fatigue at the Old Detroit stationhouse by the time Lewis and Robo-Cop returned. Robo dropped a cuffed but defiant Hob onto a bench. "You remain here," he said.

"Yeah, yeah, yeah," Hob smirked.

Robo disappeared down a hallway as Lewis slammed Officer Duffy, his hands manacled behind his back, into the booking desk. Seated behind the desk, a tired female cop named Estevez barely opened her lids wide enough to survey the scene.

Duffy was shaking, the victim of NUKE withdrawal.

Lewis reached down and yanked Hob off his bench, shoving him up against the desk as well.

Estevez glanced at the two perps. Standing together, they looked like a goose egg and a comma.

"Fun night, huh," Estevez offered.

"You got *five* minutes to let me have my phone call or my *lawyer* will have your *ass*, bitch!" Hob informed Lewis.

Unimpressed, she gently took the thumb and

forefinger of her left hand and placed them on the boy's right ear. Then she cranked the ear so hard that Hob nearly did a cartwheel. "Settle down, dumpling."

Hob placed his lips in primo-pout position. Lewis faced Estevez. "Give me a couple of minutes with Duffy here before he goes to detention."

Estevez sighed. "Lewis, you know the regulations. Put him in the tank."

"I'm feeling sick," Duffy pointed out, his face the color of seaweed.

"You know what this is, Estevez?" Lewis said, her patience wearing thin. "This is a hophead cop. He's been inside. He knows who the NUKErs are and where they are."

Estevez offered a sad smile. "Rules are rules, Lewis. I'm sorry."

Estevez's face suddenly brightened. "However," she pointed out, "regulations say that before he goes to detention he gets to use the can."

Lewis grinned at Estevez and shoved Hob into the arms of an awaiting cop. She grabbed Duffy by the shoulder and shoved him forward. "Potty time, Duff," she whispered.

As they passed Hob, the diminutive thug flashed an icy, in-control stare at Duffy. "You just keep your mouth closed," the boy advised the trembling cop, "or you'll pay."

"Go play in traffic or something, will you, squirt," Lewis said, patting an irate Hob on the head.

A gaggle of cops were clustered around the door to the station's men's room as Lewis dragged a writhing Duffy inside. Lewis eyed the other cops.

"Hey, how about giving the man a little privacy, huh?"

The cops grumbled and shuffled away.

Lewis kicked open the door to the men's room and, hauling Duff toward a stall, shoved the rotund cop butt-first into the urinal cup.

"Hey!" he said, after careful consideration.

"The NUKE, Duffy," Lewis whispered from between clenched teeth. "Who makes it and where?"

"I'm drug-dependent," Duffy said, diving into his bag of euphemisms. "Lewis, it's making me real sick. My guts don't feel so hot. My stomach is all—"

"Messed up?" Lewis slammed her left fist into the man's potbelly. Duffy doubled over with a low moan. Lewis grabbed him by the hair and yanked his head up, sending the back of it bopping into the urinal's flush button. The urinal cup filled with water. So did Duffy's pants bottom.

"C-cold!" he muttered.

"Who and *where*, you sorry sonofabitch!" Lewis said, bringing the bad cop back into the investigative loop.

The man began to sob.

Lewis didn't soften. She knew he'd crack. She had him. She had him good.

A few minutes later, Lewis stood before Sergeant Reed. Reed, a big man with a bigger temper, gazed at a spot somewhere above Lewis's head. She had seen that look before. It wasn't a good sign. She felt like a football about to tangle with a place-kicker.

"You're out of line, Lewis," Reed began, his voice

slowly gaining in volume. "That bathroom stunt you just pulled could get you *suspended*!"

Maybe it wouldn't be that bad, Lewis thought. She decided to go for it. "Just give me that assault team and you can suspend me in the morning."

"It *is* morning," Reed replied, getting up from his desk and facing a sunlit wall map. The map of Detroit was divided into sectors, with each sector subdivided into neighborhoods. Quite a few of the areas were marked with a red X.

"Are you crazy, woman?" Reed said. "We're operating with less than a *quarter* of our force."

He began jabbing the map. "We don't go to Cass Corridor . . . or Pingree Park . . . or Pole Town."

He fingered a section of the map deep in a sector the cops referred to as Forbidden Territory. "And we sure as *hell* don't go to River Rouge. We gave up on *that* shithole *before* the strike. If your NUKE gang is in there, they have to be armed to the teeth. They'll chew us up and spit us out. Body bags? We won't need them. They'll just use *doggie* bags to bring us back."

Reed faced Lewis, a pained expression on his face. "I can't risk it, Lewis. We're just going to have to wait until the strike ends."

"Sarge," Lewis pleaded, pressing home the point, "the NUKE gang *is* in there. At the old motor works. Duffy was kind enough to tell me."

"I'm sure," Reed smirked.

"Hell," Lewis continued, "they've had Duffy spilling his guts about every move we've been making for months. For sure they've got other NUKE-heads on the force. If we wait, we'll lose them for sure!"

"I'm not losing you or anybody else in a move that doesn't have a snowball's chance in hell of succ . . ." Reed stopped in midthought, gaping at the door to his office.

There, standing like a well-sculpted pillar of granite, stood RoboCop. Reed gulped. He realized that the cyborg had heard the entire conversation. "Howya doing, Robo?" he muttered.

Robo swung his body around and, turning his back on the sergeant, marched off down the corridor. Reed charged out of his office after him.

"No!" he yelled at the cyborg's back. "You are *not* going there, *mister*! That's a *direct order*!"

Robo didn't bother to slow down.

Lewis shouldered her way past her sergeant and broke into a trot. Reed grabbed her by the arm and yanked her back.

"Look, *Officer*," he said, his nostrils flaring with anger, "if *he* wants to get himself killed . . . fine. But he is *not* taking *you* with him! End of conversation!"

"But he's my partner," Lewis implored. "He might need me out there!"

"If he's going to River Rouge," Reed replied dully, "he's going to need the U.S. Marines as a partner."

Lewis nodded. Reed was right. No doubt about it: RoboCop was on a suicide mission.

11

The outskirts of the River Rouge district was a small slice of hell dropped into the remains of a once-proud city's innards. Already a slum a decade before, the area had decayed beyond that in the years since OCP had taken over the police force.

The neighborhood resembled an abandoned war zone.

Burnt-out and bombed-out tenements and storefronts stood, stretching moodily up from the bowels of the earth. The streets were pockmarked by bullets and caressed by rivers of garbage.

Hollow-cheeked transients sat bleary-eyed in what was left of the front entrances to long-abandoned dwellings.

A few wretches lined up for free meals in front of the last remaining outpost of civilization, a graffiti-stained Salvation Army establishment.

RoboCop sent his TurboCruiser purring through the mean streets. He stared at the ragged remnants of human society that inhabited the area. A twinge from deep down inside him caused him to clench his teeth.

He knew that something was happening to him.

He was evolving.

Or regressing.

He had to rein in his thoughts and . . . feelings? . . . in order to stay functional.

He must remain objective, his computer-enhanced brain advised him.

He must remain detached.

An empty bottle of Night Train smashed across the cruiser's windshield. Laughter echoed from the distance. A soft crackity-crack burst forth from a street two blocks away. Gunfire, Robo concluded.

The battered storefronts eventually gave way to wider, more desolate lots. Barren moonscapes. Never-completed excavations for buildings left unbuilt.

Weeds overran long-abandoned lots. Families once flourished here, but their houses had been torn down and never rebuilt.

Now there were only empty shells of basements left intact—bomb shelters protecting the rot and mold from the destructive rays of a deadly sun.

Robo continued to drive toward the River Rouge's old factory center: a once-thriving place where workers spent their entire lives constructing goods for an eager public, while bringing paychecks back to awaiting families. Fathers had worked the factories, and then their sons and their sons' sons.

All that was gone now.

The factories had started shutting down back in the 1980s, during the administration of an ex-B-movie actor. The national deficit had spiraled, and the country had lunged helplessly toward default.

And that, in turn, had led to the megacorporations, outfits like OCP, which had simply stepped in and taken over for the government. A loan here. A savings and loan bailout there. By the 1990s the country's government was anything but solvent, with billionaires in opulent penthouses calling the shots.

Robo sent his cruiser gliding past ancient warehouses split asunder by age, the bricks crumbling, the girders rusting, the wooden doors decaying.

He spotted no signs of human life, such as it was.

The cruiser rounded a corner. Robo eased his right foot onto the brakes. Before him loomed a series of police barriers, officially sealing off the area from law enforcement.

Dayglow graffiti was scrawled over the "OFFICIAL WARNING" signs. "GET OUTTA HERE." "POLICE AIN'T HERE, BABE." "YOU TRY, YOU DIE."

Robo clenched his teeth, pressed on the gas, and pushed the screaming cruiser into and through the barriers, leaving a spray of splintered wood in his wake.

The car proceeded to the industrial complex once known as River Rouge. At one time during the 1990s, it had been touted by an ineffectual president as "the largest industrial complex in the world." It was miles long, sleek and metallic. It had folded within the first two years of operation, when the American production industry was felled by a lethal one-two punch delivered by Japan and its eager newfound allies, the free countries of Eastern Europe.

Labor had been cheap back then abroad. At home, workers' unions had tried their best to urge for more money, more benefits.

Within a year, they'd been beaten and fragmented.

The American economy had begun to collapse, and no politician in the country could paste it back together.

Robo gazed at the River Rouge complex, sparkling like a dead fish in the harsh morning sun. Sad. Abandoned. Betrayed.

Robo's TurboCruiser was barely a speck compared with the towering, twisting, ghostly structure.

Robo's cruiser thundered over long-dead railroad tracks.

It rumbled through the shattered shell of an empty warehouse.

It rolled carefully over several side streets now inhabited by weeds and rats.

Behind the wheel, Robo scanned the desolate landscape, his RoboVision searching for something . . . anything. Any signs of life. Any signs of activity.

He gazed across row after row of factory shells. He stiffened. He trained his gaze on a powerplant partially hidden by an old TV factory.

Robo sensed the activity.

His TurboCruiser spun out of the side street, fishtailing down an alleyway toward the powerless powerplant.

Three blocks down the road, he brought the TurboCruiser to a halt. He stared at the powerplant before him. A higher chainlink fence, topped with coiled barbed wire, lined the area. Battered signs reading "HOKUSAI POWER: SALE OF WHOLE OR PART. INQUIRE: KOKIMA SAVINGS AND LOAN (312-555-6309)" and "NO TRESPASSING: UNDER PENALTY OF LAW" hung from the fence.

Robo stepped out of his cruiser and strolled up to the fence.

He scanned the area and noticed a large metal gate, still locked with a rusted padlock.

Robo marched up to the gate and grabbed the padlock.

With an effortless grunt, he yanked the padlock off the gate. He raised his right foot and sent it smashing into the gate. It toppled over with a tiny, rust-laced whimper.

Robo returned to his cruiser and gunned the engine, sending the car speeding onto the megacomplex.

High above him, four hoods stared silently at the advancing intruder. One of them motioned silently to the other three with his hand.

Below, Robo proceeded toward the power station. He tilted his head upward. Something was wrong. The car lurched into the air wildly.

Robo felt himself slammed back against the driver's seat as a land mine detonated beneath his car.

"Plastique," he muttered, watching his right rear wheel careen wildly above and beyond his windshield.

A fireball engulfed the vehicle.

Robo sighed. He had had enough of this.

Four young hoodlums appeared beyond the column of smoke belching from the ground.

Robo dove out of the car as the gas tank ignited. A mushroom cloud of flame and smoke extended an angry fist toward the sky. Robo rolled over onto the side of the road.

Within seconds, the car was nothing but a blackened shell.

The four hoods leaped through the smoke grinning, their assault rifles held high.

"Gotcha!" one of the hoods cackled.

"Not so," Robo said, arising from the grit with his gun drawn. "Throw down your weapons," he announced. "You are under arrest."

The four young hoodlums were amazed to see Robo had survived the inferno. "Last chance, creeps," Robo stated flatly.

A fifth hood appeared from the gulley behind Robo and winked at his friends. He produced a hand grenade from his pocket and, pulling the pin, heaved it at the cyborg cop. Robo had felt the heat of the hood's body and that of the weapon. He whirled around, his pistol ready, and fired two shots, one aimed high, one aimed low.

The grenade exploded in midair.

The hood exploded near ground level.

The four other hoods opened up on Robo with their assault weapons.

Feeling the lead pellets plink harmlessly off his metallic skeletal system, Robo calmly fired four times. The first thug smashed into the factory wall, his insides became outsides and, finally, a crimson graffiti stain on solid concrete.

The second punk found himself spiraling upward toward the metal stairs he had just descended.

The third dropped his gun and reached above his neck toward where his head had been not a second before. No dice. The corpse fell to the ground, still grasping for its recently departed personality.

The fourth slimeball had charged, at first not noticing that his spinal column was a memory, lying some several yards behind him. When the dawn of recognition did enter his facial features, he was too bereft of blood and muscle to do much about it. He collapsed in a heap some ten feet in front of Robo.

"Arrest would have been easier on you all," Robo opined, continuing his march toward the abandoned power station.

Robo marched into a ruptured door on the side of the power station. He entered a twilight world populated by mazes of pipes and old boilers, his Auto-9 pistol raised.

He sensed the presence of shadowshapes moving furtively above him, across a walkway. He strained his hearing capabilities. Silence. Bare feet on rusting metal.

Robo paused next to an old boiler. He scanned the area with his RoboVision, punching in the command ENHANCE AUDIO.

A tremendous hiss clouded his concentration. He spun around, raising his pistol, and faced . . . a very frightened stray cat, back arched, claws extended, defending its right to the bloodied and mangled mouse at its feet.

Robo nodded toward the cat and continued on-ward. His metallic feet sounded on the debris-strewn floor. Each clank made by his feet was deafening.

He marched up to a door. Metal. Old. Brown. He shoved it inward. The door caved in, producing a tinny sound resembling an old woman's death rat-tle.

Robo entered the entrails of the powerplant. A sudden whoosh enveloped him. A flock of pigeons, their squawks amplified even more by Robo's audio senses, erupted from the floor and flew upward, past a horror gallery of cracked and grimy win-dows.

Robo tensed his body.

He scanned the area, his RoboVision on full-alert status. Rows of long-ignored leviathan machinery loomed before him. Nothing seemed to be moving, except the pigeons, which were still squawking and defecating with glee high above him. A shadow seemed to move. Robo pivoted. A girl inhaled sharply. Robo leaned forward. A frightened sound. A sob. His RoboVision reassured him: AUDIO NORMAL.

Robo nonetheless aimed his pistol at the shadow.

No further sound.

He relaxed his stance.

From behind one of the Brobdingnagian slabs of machinery, a raven-haired girl clad in black leather and lace emerged, her arms held high above her head.

It was Angie.

"Don't shoot me!" she cried plaintively. "I'm not doing anything wrong."

"No, ma'am," Robo replied. "But please, do not move."

Robo advanced toward Angie, unaware that his head was now targeted within the precise hairs of a high-powered scope.

"I'm not doing anything wrong," Angie wailed.

Robo tried to comfort the woman as he marched forward. "I am sure you are not, ma'am," he replied.

High above the machinery, Hob crouched behind an enormous ack-ack gun fixed upon a tripod bolted to the floor. Behind him sat Cain, his legs crossed casually. Cain was grinning like the fool that, indeed, he was. He casually tapped Hob's shoulder. Hob turned to him and smiled. Cain flicked a tally-ho salute off his top hat.

Hob grinned and returned to the gun sights, prepared to squeeze the trigger.

Chivalrous Robo continued to advance toward Angie. "I am not here to do you any harm, miss," he announced. "But I would like to ask you a few questions."

Ka-pow.

Robo spun around as his left hand exploded.

Robo emitted a primal howl as sparks showered out from the stump of his wrist. The hand, still clutching its pistol, skittered around the floor in front of him.

Angie smiled at Robo. "Bull's-eye!" she declared.

Robo whirled as a young friend of Hob's, a dour-faced lad named Checkers, leaped up from behind Angie, holding a weapon of a sort Robo had never seen before.

"Howdy doooody!" said Checkers by way of greeting before firing the weapon.

A large metal ball attached to a wire slammed into Robo's chest and exploded, driving three razor-sharp prongs into his torso.

Robo staggered backward.

"Time to reel him in," Checkers declared. He worked a control on his weapon. Kzzzzzappp! Shards of electricity surged forth from a battery hooked on Checkers's belt down the wire to Robo.

Robo tilted his head back like a guillotine victim, his body twitching wildly as electrical shocks invaded his nervous system. His tongue extended from his mouth and he howled like a banshee. His body jerked like a crippled dancer as the electric shards invaded his innermost being.

Cain slid slowly down from the scaffolds above, tipping his hat toward the manic metallic cop.

Cain took a disinterested view of the situation. "Is he lunch yet?" he asked Checkers.

"Nope," Checkers replied, still cranking out power.

Hob hopped down from above, advancing on Robo's jerking body with a noncommittal look.

Robo dropped to one knee, his body still convulsing. He glanced upward at the faces of Cain, Hob, and Angie, anger welling up from within him.

Emitting a fierce, gutteral howl, he mustered up all his willpower and unhooked the prongs from his chest. Glaring at the three villains, he plunged the prongs into his wire-laden, still-sparking stump of an arm.

He grinned at the trio like a madman.

The prongs shorted in Robo's half-arm, sending a wave of electrical voltage back down the wire.

The battery at Checkers's hips immediately exploded, sending Checkers spiraling upward, his body smoldering around the midsection by the sheer power of the voltage.

Cain nodded toward the shadows.

Robo regained his footing, growling like a beast.

As he did so, the hook of a titanic iron crane crashed into his chest, sending Robo cartwheeling across the debris-strewn factory floor.

Robo twisted his clouded head, slamming into his RoboVision full tilt. A large magnet was being lowered his way. White spots flickered and flared before his eyes, along with a discouraging readout: "SYSTEMS DAMAGE ALERT! EFFICIENCY: 43% . . . 37% . . . 20% . . ."

Robo blanked out as the titanic magnet connected to his chest. Robo was lifted from the floor by the magnetic force as the metal beast drew him into its grasp with a resounding clank. The magnet lifted the inert RoboCop high into the air.

In the cab of the gigantic crane, the gorilla henchman Catzo guided the magnet home.

Cain walked cheerfully alongside the magnet as it hoisted Robo toward destinations unknown. Cain paused to help Checkers to his feet.

"Are you all right?"

"Yeah." The kid nodded. "I have a bad stomachache, though. Shithead cop doesn't play fair."

"Cops never do, lad," Cain replied.

Checkers nodded and limped away. Cain glared at Robo as the magnet lowered him onto steel runners.

Checkers, Angie, and a thug named Gillette pulled heavy metal clamps across Robo's body, pinning his arms and legs effectively down on the runners. The magnet spiraled harmlessly away into the sky.

Robo's head began to sway back and forth.

He shook his senses clear. Enraged at his predicament, he began to thrash around, growling, howling, snarling.

"Temper, temper," Cain advised, tilting his hat down jauntily over his left eye.

A small army of thugs converged above Robo. One of them hauled up a jackhammer. Another produced a lethal electric drill. Yet another wielded an acetylene torch. All three stood poised, ready to start the robotics operation ordered by Cain.

Cain lowered himself above Robo's silent gaze. "I don't blame you for this," Cain acknowledged. "I know you don't have any choice. They program you, and you do it. But you've upset a delicate balance in my agenda, my life-style. We can't let the police come here. It's just not possible."

Cain raised his skeletal form in a sudden wave of rage. "I don't blame you. And I know you can't help but blame me!"

He smiled sweetly down at the prone cyborg. "But, rest assured, I forgive you for that."

Cain lifted a large lug wrench with both hands and swung it down onto Robo's head. Wham! Again and again and again. Wham! Wham! Wham! Cain emitted a primordial howl as he continued to send the wrench slamming down into Robo's sleek helmeted head. Again. Again. Again. More! More! More! Destroy! Destroy! Destroy!

Finally Cain stopped, sobbing.

Angie moved forward to comfort her distraught leader.

He shook her away, gazing down at the stunned RoboCop.

"Good-bye," he sobbed. "Good-bye."

Robo stared toward the ceiling of the factory, wide-eyed. He was paralyzed. His senses whirled helplessly as Cain backed away, dropping his wrench and waving the other hoods forward.

Jackhammer.

In the gut.

Robo screamed.

Robo passed out before the torches and the drills began their dance of death.

12

As dusk fell, the police picket lines surrounding the Old Detroit stationhouse were bathed in a blood-red glow. Chanting and holding their signs high, the police mood of solidarity was fractured by the screeching tires of an approaching limousine.

The limo careened to a halt, and its rear door opened.

The cops turned as one as the sound of metal on concrete reverberated in their ears.

A hapless hunk of metal was tossed onto the street, the limo speeding off after the deed was done.

The cops, led by a man named Whittaker, ran up to the mangled heap of metal.

Whittaker grabbed the hulk and turned it over. It was RoboCop. His legs and arms were connected to his torso by threads. His eyes stared blankly at the orange sky above. There were no signs of life, of vitality.

"My God!" Whittaker whispered. "He's been stripped to the bone!"

The striking cops behind him exchanged guilty glances.

To a man, the cops threw down their picket signs and converged on the mangled metallic shell.

They carried Robo into the station as if they were at an official police funeral.

Within the station, there was silence.

An hour went by. The city went to hell.

Within two hours, life was back to normal.

Inside the stationhouse, there was the usual in-strike chaos. Phones rang off the hook. Terrified temps regarded the phones as if they were vipers, poised for a lethal bite. Reed was at his desk, screaming into the phone. An old bloodied woman sitting on a chair near the front desk babbled.

"But Robert doesn't eat nothing," she declared. "Just eats what he eats and doesn't change his clothes or say nothing."

"Gawd!" a nearby temp exclaimed. "And he has a knife? What're you going to do? What? Me? Hell? I don't give advice. I'm no cop."

Reed barked into his phone. "Try to stay calm, ma'am. That police lock will keep them out. Did you get a good look at them? That's all right, ma'am. Just try to stay calm. A squad car will be along as soon as possible. Now, if you could just hold . . . Yes, ma'am. Some of us are still working. . . . Thank you, ma'am. We love you, too."

Lewis appeared before Reed's desk and slammed her left fist onto its top. "REED!"

Reed cupped the phone. "What the hell are you doing here, Lewis? It's not your shift."

Lewis practically snarled at the hapless sergeant. "I *heard* about what happened to Murphy, Reed. And I'm holding *you* personally responsible!"

She glared at Reed for a moment before she stormed off. Another phone rang. Reed sighed and picked it up. "Metro North. Yeah, this is the police. *Yes, there are still police!*"

Lewis made her way to the dark dank Robo-Chamber. Upon entering the cubicle, she stopped cold, her eyes widened in terror.

Robo sat upon his perch.

His eyes were wide open but bereft of life. He stared blankly into space. Robo's torso hung suspended by pulleys, vital fluids dripping from its innards. His helmet was gone. A puppet's mask encased by circuitry was all that was left of his once beautiful face. Life-support tubes and wires hung suspended from his exposed sockets. Tak Akita and Linda Garcia ran frantically from high-tech machine to machine.

"Is he alive?" Lewis asked.

"The cerebro spinal axis is viable," Tak admitted, "but all circuits interfacing with the medulla spinalis are shot to shit."

Lewis felt tears brimming in her eyes. "Please, in English. *Is . . . he . . . alive?*"

Garcia sighed and faced the lady cop. "His brain is . . . well, we're still getting a signal from it. It's faint. If we can keep it going, maybe we can rebuild him."

"Maybe?" Lewis repeated.

"If we can get the parts," Tak said. "Which, thanks to OCP's budget cutbacks, doesn't seem likely."

Lewis narrowed her eyes. "What the hell do you mean? Is OCP up to some new shit?"

Tak shrugged. "They said he's off warranty."

"Off warranty?" Lewis exclaimed.

"They've put a hold on sending any replacements," Garcia tried to explain.

Lewis blew up. "He's not just some piece of *equipment*, damnit! He's my fuggin' partner!"

"Hey," said Garcia softly, "I'm not arguing with you. We're doing everything we can."

Lewis felt her heart break and her body sag. "I know. I'm sorry. Can you give me a list of what it'll take to fix him?"

"What's the point?" Garcia muttered. "OCP won't spring for the damned—"

"Just make me the list," Lewis said flatly.

"It'll be ready in an hour," Garcia replied, flashing a sympathetic grin.

Lewis strode past the two flustered robotics experts and leaned close to Robo's frozen face. "Just hold on, honey," she said, her lips nearly touching his. "We're gonna fix you."

Lewis turned her back on the scientists and left the room.

"That lady's crazy," Tak declared.

"Yeah." Garcia nodded.

"She's beyond crazy," Tak added.

Garcia smiled. "So you like her, too?"

Tak focused a mournful look on Robo. "Yeah, goddamnit, I like her a *lot*."

Lewis left the RoboChamber, tears in her eyes. She entered the main room of the stationhouse and stopped with a start. Behind his desk, Reed was conversing with a bleary-eyed, heavily sedated Officer Duffy. Duffy was led past the desk by a badly suited attorney who resembled a wharf rat in polyester.

Duffy reeled to a halt in front of Lewis. "Hiya, sweetcakes! Good to see ya."

His lawyer led him away.

Lewis spun on Reed. "Sarge? What the hell is this crap?"

Reed faced her impassively. "What the hell do you *expect*, Lewis? You don't read him his *rights*, you *punch* a confession out of him, and you think we can *hold* him?"

Duffy chuckled, winking at Lewis. "You're lucky I'm such a nice guy. I could've had your badge for you fuggin' me up."

Reed glared at the rodent attorney. "Go on. Get him out of here."

The little man nodded and yanked Duffy away. Reed spun on Lewis. "Nice work, *Officer*."

"Perch and rotate, Sarge," Lewis said, striding out of the station. "I've got other things to think about."

"Don't you dare!" Reed roared. "There is a time and a place for everything."

"Screw off," Lewis whispered.

"What!" Reed demanded.

"I said, 'hoooo-offff.' Think I'm catching a cold."

"You're gonna catch hell if you start messing around with robotics and OCP junk and politics and stuff I don't know and don't want to know."

"Would I do a thing like that?" Lewis called over her shoulder, slamming through the front doors of the station.

13

The stretch limo pulled up silently before the hospital. A pale green moon shone down upon the scene.

The angular and obviously angry figure of Cain emerged from the back. The equally tall but angelic-looking thug named Gillette walked around the back. Together they hauled the unconscious, still-uniformed body of Officer Duffy out of the trunk and slowly dragged him into the emergency room.

Inside the green-walled hospital, Duffy was stripped, sedated, and tossed upon a gurney.

Expressionless attendants wheeled Duffy into an operating room.

The gorilla, Catzo, dismissed the attendants, pushing a medical cart into the center of the room. Duffy was strapped to a table, his rotund body covered by a sheet. Duffy began to regain consciousness ever so slowly.

His face was badly bruised.

Badly beaten.

His eyes were nearly swollen shut.

He tried to focus his eyes on the harsh ceiling lights. He cocked his ears. Footsteps. Growing nearer. And nearer. And nearer. His body tensed.

Cain and Angie entered the room, both wearing medical garb. Angie walked placidly over to another medical cart.

Catzo left the room.

Cain sidled up to Duffy, beaming in his doctor's outfit. "I can't believe you told the cops where I was headquartered, Duffy. I just can't believe it. You, a man of *honor*. A man who wears the *badge*."

Duffy tried to summon a smile. "I didn't. That's not *true*. Oh, Cain! Jeeezus! It's not *true*."

Cain nodded and chuckled. He glanced at Angie. "Our boy's lying again, Angie."

Angie shrugged.

The smile faded from Cain's face. "He's lying to *me*!"

Angie turned to Duffy. "A shame, really," she said demurely. "All that bitch had to do was sit you in a urinal and punch you in the gut? And you told them where we *were*? We know all about it, Duffy. You think you're the only cop we have under our thumb?"

Angie turned her back on the captive cop. She removed the covering from her cart. It was laden with surgical instruments straight out of *Bride of Frankenstein*. The overhead lights made their long, sharp surfaces glisten. Duffy began to whimper. Cain offered him a sincere smile of condolence.

"Sorry, bub." He grinned.

"Oh, God! Oh, Jeeezus," Duffy moaned. "I am truly sorry!"

Cain shrugged his skeletal shoulders, rubbing his right hand through his half-grown beard. "It really hurts me that you did what you did," he said. "It really caused me a lot of pain."

He turned to Angie, who was fingering the tools. "Stop that! You'll hurt yourself."

Duffy ignored the last blast. "Don't *kill* me, Cain. I'm begging you, man. I'll do *anything*. ANYTHING!"

Cain smiled sweetly. "I don't believe in revenge, Duffy. I'd even let you go if I could. But my life . . . ah, well, it isn't all that simple. I don't have the kind of freedom most people have. So many depend on me. . . . And you, through your stupidity, have endangered them all."

"Please don't kill me," Duffy moaned, his body still strapped down onto the table.

Cain retreated. He sat in a large chair.

Angie ran to his side, crouching and stroking him. He nodded at her serenely before facing Duffy.

"No, I won't kill you," he intoned. "I don't kill. I never kill."

An unshaven, middle-aged fat man stumbled into the room. He donned surgical gloves. Angie smiled and handed Cain a NUKE dispenser. Cain smiled and picked an ampule. He handed it to the fat man. The fat man plunged it into his neck and turned toward Duffy.

"No," Cain said again, "I never kill. I have people who can do that for me."

The fat man stared wild-eyed at Duffy.

He raised a scalpel.

Within the blink of an eye, he had sliced Duffy's sheet open.

Duffy sighed. His skin wasn't broken.

The fat man picked up another scalpel, his eyes rotating wildly.

Cain watched placidly as the second scalpel slid into Duffy's ample flesh. He averted his eyes as the cop began to scream.

Angie merely ignored the scene. She plunged a NUKE ampule into her neck and watched the operation while in a blissful state of dull fascination.

Cain continued to watch the carving. What the hell? There was nothing decent on cable these days.

14

The Old Detroit stationhouse was illuminated by a smog–dimmed moonlight glow.

Behind the desk sat a haggard Officer Estevez, as battered cops dropped coins and bills into a cigarbox while either leaving or coming home from their extended tours of duty. Reed marched into the room. Estevez nodded and scrambled out of the seat. She quickly donned her suit of armor.

"Night duty?" Reed asked.

"No," she sneered, producing a couple of dollar bills and plunking them into the cigarbox. "I'm off to the senior prom."

Reed nodded placidly.

A rookie cop, his face blood-stained, waddled into the room. He stared at the box. "This for Robo?"

Reed nodded. "Yeah," he acknowledged. "Lewis figures if we've got the money, OCP has got to give us the parts."

The rookie slammed his money into the box and staggered off.

Estevez faced Reed angrily. "Shit!" she exclaimed. "They don't give a good god*damn* about Robo—or *any* of us! They pulled this same shit on me when I hurt my knee. They said they were suspending medical benefits until they could accurately ascertain—"

"You want a collection, too, Estevez?" Reed inquired.

"Nossir," Estevez hissed. "I've never been hurt as much as that boy in there. It's as bad as ripping out a person's heart, goddamnit!"

Reed lapsed into silence.

He stared at the front door as a contrite figure entered the room. Whittaker, the leader of the police strike force, held his cop hat in his hand. It was filled with money.

Reed glared at the striking cop. "Only working cops allowed in here, Whittaker."

Estevez managed a snarl. "Back to your picket line, you limp-wristed dick."

Whittaker ignored it all as he continued marching forward to Reed's desk. He dumped his hatful of money into the cigarbox before the officer and stared at him sullenly.

"Do me a small favor, Sarge," he whispered. "Tell Robo that the guys on the line are thinking about him, rooting for him. I only hope this'll help. We're *all* still cops, bejeezus, inside and outside this station."

Whittaker turned and marched out of the building.

Reed stared at the money in the box. "Well, I'll be goddamned," he muttered.

The cops in the stationhouse fell into silence.

Even the criminals in the holding cell seemed to have been affected.

Estevez donned her helmet. "Now, if there's no more sob stories to slobber over, I'm going out onto the streets."

"Be careful out there," Reed warned.

"Always am," Estevez said. "I mean, who cares about cops any more, eh?"

"Only other cops," Reed whispered.

15

Sunlight glistened through the massive skylights at the Old Man's private penthouse suite at OCP. A switch was flicked. Golden blinds closed out the sunlight.

The Old Man, in a deep Japanese bathtub, placed a wet finger on a set of high-tech computerized controls. He frowned slightly as the sound of knocking invaded his private chambers.

The Old Man sighed. "Yes, Johnson. Come in. Come in."

Johnson appeared in the portal as the two gigantic golden doors automatically swung inward. He glanced about. The room was littered with lush, tropical plants. The Old Man tilted his head back into the tub, relaxed and confident.

Johnson ventured forward. "Good morning, sir."

"Good morning, Johnson." The Old Man sighed. "What is it?"

"I'm sorry to bother you this early," Johnson began, his glasses fogging from the steam of the tub.

"But . . ." said the Old Man.

"But," Johnson continued, "I think we could be facing a serious crisis."

The Old Man nodded above the swirling waters. "Well," he ventured, "I think that, over the years, I've learned that crises come and crises go. What's all this about, huh, Johnson, my dear boy?"

"It's all flummoxed," Johnson admitted.

"How so?"

"Our position on RoboCop: It's becoming a severe public-relations problem. All six networks are going after us for keeping RoboCop offline."

The Old Man nodded, blowing bubbles away from his mouth.

Johnson gritted his teeth and continued. "Now, I know that Doctor Faxx feels it's time to phase out the existing RoboCop. And with her marketing experience, you'd think she would be aware of the damage she's doing to our corporate image."

Faxx, a small clinging towel her only clothing, entered the scene from an ajoining bedroom, well out of Johnson's line of view. "But," the poor executive continued, "I really have to question the wisdom of having her in charge of the RoboCop 2 program. I'm worried she may have some agenda of her own that's not in synch with this company."

Johnson nearly gagged as the scantily clad Dr. Faxx strutted out before him.

"And what would that agenda be, dear Mr. Johnson?" she cooed, almost exposing her breasts to him with a quick slip of her towel.

Johnson opened and closed his mouth, producing a mere hummuna-hummuna-hummmmmmuna sound.

Faxx let her towel slip lower. "The fact is that I'm well aware of the image problem we have with RoboCop. And I have a solution."

The Old Man chortled from his bath. "Yes, Johnson. Juliette and I have already discussed it. I'll be counting on you, dear sir, to help implement her ideas."

Johnson heaved a dry cough. He felt his bowels trying to strain free. "Of course. Whatever I can do."

The Old Man raised a rubber-duckie toy from the bubbles. "Anything else, *boy*?"

Johnson turned his head right and left, like the slave he truly was. "No," he muttered. "Nothing else."

Johnson glared at the woman. He wished her dead.

The Old Man slid further into the tub, taking his duckie with him. "Good." He smiled. "And now, if you would be so kind as to close the door on your way out."

Johnson casually daubbed the sweat off his face and backed toward the two towering exit doors. He banged his back against them and left the room, almost in a near bow.

As the doors swung closed, Juliette Faxx dropped her towel and glided into the tub alongside the Old Man. The Old Man smiled, nearly drooling at her.

Within seconds, his rubber duckie had been tossed from the watery scene.

16

Dr. Juliette Faxx sat quietly in her office, surveying the sunlit skyline before her. Two low-level robotics experts stood nervously nearby, holding several large drawings of state-of-the-art weaponry in their hands. Faxx purposely ignored them. Behind her, her administrative assistant, Jenny, appeared in the doorway.

"Officer Lewis is here," Jenny announced.

Faxx nodded and spun her chair around as Officer Anne Lewis, dressed in civilian clothes, entered the room. She carried a thick stack of printouts under her arm.

Faxx said nothing as she motioned Lewis in with a wave of her hand.

Faxx turned to the sweating executives. "Very striking, gentlemen," she murmured. "I'm sure the Pentagon would consider it if you could bring the unit cost down three hundred and fifty million. That will be all."

The two execs backed out of the room like frightened mice. Lewis stood awkwardly before Faxx's desk.

"Please"—Faxx smiled at her—"sit down."

Lewis eased herself into a chair.

Faxx eyed the printouts. "Sorry to keep you waiting, Officer. That's not the *list*, is it?"

Lewis nodded mutely.

Faxx was handed the printouts, and she began to leaf through them. "I had no idea the damage was so extensive."

"We've collected money," Lewis offered. "If it's not enough, we'll collect more."

"How much money?" Faxx asked.

"A couple thousand bucks," Lewis admitted. "But that's only from two precincts."

Faxx smiled thinly. "I'm afraid a 'couple thousand bucks' won't do it. His helmet alone costs . . . oh, never mind."

Lewis's face reddened. She rose from her chair. "Look, I'll get more. Tell me how much and I'll get it."

Faxx leaned back in her chair. "Please Officer, relax."

She smiled warmly at Lewis as the cop slid back down into her chair.

"I was able to convince my superiors that we could not abandon our company's finest achievement," Faxx cooed. "You'll get the parts, along with a crack technical team . . . and a program update I'm preparing myself."

Lewis gaped at the executive. "You're gonna fix him?"

Faxx grinned. "We're gonna fix him."

Tears welled up in Lewis's eyes. "Thank you, Doctor. Thank you."

Faxx nodded, still radiating a warm smile. "We *all* love him around here, you know. I can tell you feel something special about him yourself."

"He's my partner," Lewis said. "With cops, that means a lot."

"You're a very caring person," Faxx commented. "That's much more important than grace or intelligence to many people."

Lewis shook her head clear. She'd just been verbally sucker-punched and she knew it. She wanted to get angry but was too confused to light the spark. She slowly arose from her chair. Faxx followed the move, leaning over her desk and grasping Lewis by the hand.

"We'll begin immediately." The doctor smiled. "Why don't you start spreading the good word?"

Lewis nodded and, slightly light-headed, walked out of the room. She didn't know what the hell had just gone down in Faxx's office.

When the policewoman was gone, Faxx pushed an intercom button. "It's done. I'll be right up."

She walked to the door and waited until she saw Lewis enter a descending elevator before she left her office.

Minutes later, in an OCP conference room, the cool Dr. Faxx chatted with a group of company executives, including a frowning Johnson.

"RoboCop's command program," she began, "his set of directives, determines his behavior. It's time to update that program, and I'd like to hear from each and every one of you."

The flattered executives glanced at each other. At Faxx's side, Jenny prepared to take notes.

A female executive leaned forward. "I've always thought that RoboCop should relate more sympathetically to women."

Faxx nodded. "Interesting. Thank you."

"He's always making such value judgments," a bald-headed sleazeball declared. "I think what we need is a value-neutral RoboCop."

"Very good," Faxx commented.

"Couldn't he take a little time to address environmental issues?" one newcomer asked.

"I don't see any reason why not," Faxx agreed.

"And all that shooting he does," a second woman exec moaned. "I've never once seen him take the time to do something *nice*. Like visit an orphanage!"

Johnson sighed. "Or help a cat out of a tree," he added sarcastically. "Or go door to door, collecting for the Red Cross."

Faxx shot Johnson an icy grin. "Very good, Mr. Johnson. The media would love that. Thank you so much."

Johnson sunk lower in his seat as the round-robin suggestion period droned on.

Why don't you just cut him up completely? Johnson thought to himself. *That's all you want to do anyhow.*

17

Sergeant Reed clutched his head in his hands as he sat behind his desk. Before him, two dozen perps were waiting to be booked. Half a dozen cops had been shot in the past two days. The crisis on the streets of Detroit was worsening every hour.

He pushed his blotter aside and stalked into the corridors behind his desk, a frazzled Officer Estevez at his side.

"This isn't police work," he fumed. "This is *shit*, Estevez. The entire city is becoming unglued. Parkhouse just called from Grosse Pointe, begging for help."

"Grosse Pointe?" Estevez blinked. "But that's a money neighborhood! Since when do they need help from us?"

"They've lost two cops there in the last forty-eight hours," he grumbled. "A bunch of kids used a goddamned grenade launcher on them. It's a jungle now, like everywhere else."

Reed turned to Estevez. "Man the front desk for me, will ya?"

Estevez nodded and returned to the main room of the stationhouse. Reed clomped into the Robo-Chamber.

A freshly reconstituted RoboCop sat serenely in his throne. Helmet securely in place, the repaired Robo looked good as new. Tak Akita and Linda Garcia manned the computer console, running tests.

Robo's hands flexed.

His head turned.

His legs pumped up and down casually.

Reed stared at the two robotics experts. "He was supposed to be ready an hour ago. All hell is breaking loose outside. Is something wrong?"

"No," Tak replied, punching his keypads. "It's the new command program from OCP. It's a big one. It's taking forever to download."

"Done," Garcia declared.

Reed turned to RoboCop. The mighty metal cop slowly arose from his throne and turned to Reed.

The sergeant grinned. "How are you feeling, Murphy?"

Robo flashed Reed a sincere grin. "I am just fine, Bill. Golly. Thanks for asking."

Robo left the room, a new bounce to his step. Reed shot a bewildered glance at the two robotics experts. They blinked, totally baffled.

Robo exited the police station, waving cheerfully at the picketing cops. "Good morning," he chirped.

"Whuttha?" the cop named Whittaker exclaimed.

A half-hour later, a burglary alarm cut through the silence of a slow day. Shouts echoed through the streets, joined by the sound of breaking glass.

The elderly owner of an electronics store staggered across his showroom, his head bleeding. He ducked as equipment sailed through the air, barely missing his already fractured skull. A young punk wearing a Motor City Muskrats baseball uniform cackled as he leaped onto a counter and began emptying the cash register.

"Please," the old man begged.

"Fuck you," the kid giggled, stuffing the money into his pockets.

Half a dozen other small fry, also clad in baseball uniforms, bashed opulent electronics displays with little-league baseball bats. They gathered high-tech electronics merchandise and hauled it toward the front door.

Their stoned-out adult coach followed, carrying a large video monitor.

"Let's go," called the coach. "The NUKE's on me."

The coach and the team stumbled out onto the streets, carrying their merchandise to the back of a small gray van. They began loading the booty into the van when the coach froze in his tracks. He whipped out a pistol as a police TurboCruiser glided down the street.

"Cheeze it!" he yelped. "Cops!"

He fired a round at the approaching cruiser.

Anne Lewis ducked as the bullet shattered the windshield. She tumbled from the cruiser and rolled on the ground as the demented coach fired round after round in her direction.

Lewis crawled to the back of the cruiser, taking cover and drawing her own weapon.

Still seated behind the wheel was a cool, calm, and collected RoboCop.

He slowly emerged from the vehicle, the coach still firing.

"Shit, guys!" one little slugger declared. "It's RoboCop!"

The kids stopped loading the stolen goods and, as one, raised their hands high into the air.

Robo stood next to the cruiser, inert.

Lewis crouched behind him, taking cover behind his metallic form.

The coach continued firing.

Lewis heard the bullets zing off Robo's torso.

"Come on, Murph!" she hissed. "Wake up already! Do something!"

Robo remained in place.

The coach continued firing.

Lewis raised her gun.

The coach stopped firing.

The coach stopped breathing.

The coach stopped living. He tumbled down onto the ground with a thud. Half of his team ran back into the store.

"Let's hit the rear!" one kid advised.

Lewis darted out from behind Robo. "Thanks for the help, partner. I really appreciate it."

The six sluggers raced to the rear of the building and began grappling with the back door. It was locked. They turned to run toward the entrance and found their path blocked by a very disgruntled Lewis, her gun pointed in their direction.

"Out front, munchkins. Now!"

Lewis led the kids out of the store and tossed them up against the storefront.

Robo lifted the lifeless coach's body high into the air and gazed at it. "You are under arrest," he announced.

"He's dead, Murphy," Lewis called from over her shoulder.

"You have the right to remain silent," Robo advised the corpse.

"Safe bet he's gonna take that advice," Lewis called.

"You have the right to an attorney," Robo shouted at the body. Flies were already gathering at the cadaver's bleeding nose.

"You're reading the *Miranda* warning to a corpse, Murphy!" Lewis shouted.

Robo glanced at Lewis, then he stared at the body. He dropped it. "Sorry," he muttered. "I am having . . . trouble."

Robo glanced at the young baseball team of felons. Through his RoboVision he saw a new directive. CHILDREN PRESENT. ROLE MODEL MODE. DIRECTIVE SEVEN: PROMOTE CIVIC PRIDE. DIRECTIVE NINE: RESTRAIN HOSTILE FEELINGS. DIRECTIVE FOURTEEN: SEEK NONVIOLENT SOLUTIONS.

Robo grinned and, pushing Lewis to the side, gathered the children together, just at the point when the bloodied owner staggered out of the shop. Robo pointed toward the battered storefront.

"Now, kids," Robo began, "that was not nice."

Lewis and the store owner exchanged startled glances.

The kids lapsed into a state of shock.

Robo continued to lecture the children, his face betraying several nervous tics as he spoke, his body convulsing slightly as well.

"You see, destructive behavior breeds . . ."

Robo's head jerked.

"Have a nice . . ."

His lips twitched.

"You cannot make an omelet without breaking a few . . . eggs . . . eggs . . ."

One kid turned to another. "Shit. This guy is *really* fucked up."

"Bad language," Robo began, "makes for bad . . . bad . . . feelings."

"Let's blow this popstand," one slugger advised the pack.

The kids sprinted away from Robo, past Lewis and down the street.

"They're getting away!" the store owner moaned.

He turned to Robo, shaking violently. "You let them get away! What the hell is wrong with you!"

"Gosh," Robo replied. "You seem hostile."

"Hostile?" the owner snarled. "They wrecked my shop and you give them a Captain Kangaroo lecture! You stupid metal bastard, I oughtta—"

Robo lifted the store owner high into the air by his throat. The man began to choke.

"And you have a nice day too, sir." Robo smiled, dropping the merchant onto the ground like a ton of bricks.

Robo sauntered back to the cruiser and climbed behind the wheel. "Coming, Annie?" he called.

Officer Lewis, more than confused, nodded and climbed in beside him. "Where to, Murphy-urphy?"

"Where destiny leads us," Robo said, sending the cruiser back onto the streets—at a good twenty miles an hour.

After a few minutes of cruising in molasses time, Lewis grew impatient. "Hit the gas, Murphy! People raise families in less time than it's taking us to move across the sector."

"The posted limit is thirty-five," Robo cautioned. "I must set a good example for the populace, Annie."

"Annie my fanny!" Lewis groused. "Nobody has called me that since I was nine, and besides, you never . . . you never!"

She faced Robo. "Murphy! You would never call me that! It's OCP again, isn't it? They did something to you, didn't they? They messed with your mind."

Robo continued to drive. "I am fine. And have I told you that your hair looks lovely that way?"

Lewis slinked down into her seat. "Oh, gee, thanks."

"And the moon is pretty tonight, is it not?" Robo continued.

"It's broad daylight," Lewis pointed out.

"Does not matter," Robo replied. "It is the thought that counts."

"Jesus!" Lewis sighed. "We're heading back to the station. That's all there is to—"

Robo slammed on the cruiser's brakes. Lewis

lurched forward, her face slamming into the dashboard. "Awww, Jesusfugginchristmas, Murphy!" she howled. "You almost broke my goddamn face in!"

Robo exited the car silently.

He walked toward a group of slum children cavorting around an open fire hydrant. Robo walked into the geyser of water and reached down toward the hydrant. Using his hand, he twisted the hydrant closed.

The little kids stood there startled.

"What's that for?" one kid demanded. "We wuz only havin' a little fun. We can't afford to go to no OCP pool or nuthin'."

Robo faced the children. "Conserving our natural resources is everybody's . . ."

His body jerked.

"A rolling stone . . ."

He jerked again.

". . . is worth two in the bush."

He jerked a third time.

". . . except after *c*."

The kids giggled at the spastic RoboCop. One older kid crept up behind him and, whipping out a can of spray paint, wrote "kick me" on Robo's back.

"Awww, go fuck a refrigerator, pecker neck," one little girl declared.

"Bad language makes for bad feelings," Robo instructed her.

The little girl turned to face Robo, who bent nearer. The child let go with a massive belch.

"And one must always pay attention to one's

diet," Robo continued as the older kid with the spray can painted over Robo's visor.

Robo stood perplexed as a small gaggle of adult citizens gathered and began to howl with laughter as the kids continued to badger the metallic minion of the law.

Lewis exited the car and trotted over, brandishing her gun. "All right, jerk-offs. The show's over. Break it up before I break some butt."

"Bitch!" a little girl hissed, stalking off.

Lewis extended a foot.

The little hellion tripped over the extended boot and fell facedown into a puddle.

"Clumsy you." Lewis grinned at the little devil. She took Robo by the hand and led him toward the car.

Suddenly Robo stiffened. He wheeled around, whipping out his gun.

Lewis cringed as three shots belched out of Robo's massive handgun.

On the far side of the street, a man smoking a cigarette fell back against a wall, Robo's bullets neatly encircling his head.

The man, wide-eyed with terror, opened his mouth in a silent scream. The cigarette dangled for a moment from his lower lip, before tumbling onto the ground before his feet.

Robo holstered his gun and waved at the man. "Thank you for not smoking," he called.

Lewis took Robo by the hand and led him back to the cruiser. "You sit in the passenger's seat," she advised. "I'll drive."

"But why?" Robo asked.

"You brake for animals?" Lewis asked.

"But of course," Robo answered.

"You stay in the right lane of the road except for when it's necessary to pass?" Lewis countered.

"Of course," Robo replied.

"From now on," said Lewis firmly, "until we get you to a good robotic shrink, I'm driving, I'm making the calls, and I'm pulling the collars."

"Whatever you say, Officer Lewis. I am not a sexist, you know."

"I know."

"And by the way, have I told you your hair looks lovely that way?"

"Yes." Lewis sighed, easing the cruiser forward. "You have."

Robo nodded contentedly. "I thought I had."

18

RoboCop sat placidly on his throne, his helmet in place, his face relaxed. A thick computer cable ran from the base of his skull into the base of his throne. Linda Garcia, muttering curses under her breath, slowly wiped the spray paint from his visor. Tak Akita motioned a concerned Lewis toward a computer monitor.

More and more directives scrolled out onto the screen.

DIRECTIVE 233: RESTRAIN HOSTILE FEELINGS.

DIRECTIVE 234: PROMOTE POSITIVE ATTITUDES.

DIRECTIVE 235: SUPPRESS AGGRESSIVE EMOTIONS.

DIRECTIVE 236: PROMOTE SOCIAL VALUES.

DIRECTIVE 237: ENCOURAGE ENVIRONMENTAL CONSCIOUSNESS.

DIRECTIVE 238: AVOID DESTRUCTIVE BEHAVIOR.

DIRECTIVE 239: BE ACCESSIBLE TO THE PUBLIC.

DIRECTIVE 240: PARTICIPATE IN GROUP ACTIVITIES.

DIRECTIVE 241: AVOID INTERPERSONAL CONFLICTS.

The scroll of robotic *dos* and *don'ts* continued. Lewis frowned. "What the *hell* is all that stuff?"

"New directives," Tak answered. "Directed toward the Robo command system. There are hundreds of them. The poor bastard must be going out of his mind."

Garcia nodded, still wiping off the paint. "It's not like he can just say *no*. They've put all this nonsense into his *brain*. He *has* to *obey*. That's the way he's made."

"Take them out," Lewis ordered. "*All* of them!"

"We can't." Tak sighed. "Not here. Not with the equipment we're allowed. I'm afraid he'll have to stay this way until OCP sees fit to fix him."

"They're the ones who did this to him!" Lewis was fuming. "We won't get any help from them. You know that, Tak."

"Anne," said Tak sadly, "there's nothing I can do. I'm sorry."

"Are you telling me there's no way to bring Robo back?" Lewis asked. "I can't believe that."

"Sure, there are ways," Tak conceded. "You could pull his cranial circuits out, which would shut down his life-support system altogether. . . ."

Garcia climbed down from her perch next to the throne. "Or you could run a few thousand volts through him and pray his insulation holds out and his living tissue doesn't get fried."

"Whatever we do," Tak said, "it would be too big a gamble. We could destroy him."

"*Kill* him?" Lewis gasped.

"*Destroy* him if you believe he's a machine," Tak stated. "*Kill* him if you believe he is a thinking, human being."

Robo lurched to life.

"What the fu—" Tak began.

Robo ripped the cable from his head. All the readout screens on the computer consoles went blank.

"Hey, hold on there!" Garcia screamed.

Robo glanced at Tak, Garcia, and Lewis. His eyes were cold and steely.

He arose from his throne and walked out of the room.

Lewis tried to follow. "Hey! Murphy! Where the hell do you think you're going?"

Robo marched ahead of Anne Lewis, shoving startled policemen and -women out of his way.

He hit the front exit at a full canter and continued to the street.

Lewis skittered to a stop at the front door. "Oh, Murphy," she whispered. "Poor Murphy. You've been through so much. Come back to us, Murph. Come back. We're your family now. Realize that. Believe that. Come back. We love you, you big bag of bolts."

19

Outside the stationhouse, Robo waved to the pick-eting police officers as he walked toward the side of the building. Whittaker turned to a cop named Stef. "Murphy's gone out of his *mind*." He sighed. "He went into the juvenile tank this morning. The way I heard it, he gave them an hour-long lecture on civics."

"Way I figure it," Stef smirked, "it's just one less scab to worry about. Management will cave in that much quicker."

"Hey," Whittaker protested, "Murphy's no scab."

"Am I *missing* something here, Whittaker?" Stef asked. "I don't recall him marching on this picket line."

"He's a *machine*, Stef," Whittaker said. "They *tell* him what to do."

"So, how is it he can go crazy then, smartass?" Stef retorted. "How does a machine go nuts? He's a fucking scab, plain and simple."

"Hey, what's going on, there?" Whittaker wondered aloud.

Robo had paused in his march, staring down the alleyway next to the side of the stationhouse. He then began to walk down the alley. Whittaker motioned for Stef and a few other cops to leave the picket line. They followed Robo's path.

"What the hell is he up to?" Whittaker asked.

"You're asking me?" Stef smirked. "You're the expert on machines."

Robo walked up to a large transformer at the side of the station. A chainlink fence surrounded it, reading "DANGER: HIGH VOLTAGE." Robo extended his hands, grabbed the fence, and tore it asunder.

Then he grabbed the protective metal covering of the transformer and tore that away as well.

"Hey!" Stef called. "Get away from there, Murphy. That thing's *dangerous!*"

Without warning, Robo thrust his hands into the transformer.

The cops near him shielded their eyes as an explosion of sparks ripped through the alleyway.

Robo's body twitched as angry fingers of blue lightning zapped out of the transformer and into his body.

He tilted his head back and screamed as part of his wiring burst into flames.

Robo emitted a deafening howl as the electricity continued to invade his system.

Lewis ran out of the stationhouse and skidded around to the alley.

Robo stood there screeching in pain.

"Murphy!" Lewis gasped, running down the alley

and past the small gaggle of cops. She made a beeline for the twitching, tortured RoboCop.

"Don't touch him, Lewis," Stef urged, running after her and downing her with a flying tackle.

"What the hell is going on here?" one of the picketers in front of the building asked. "Holy shit! Officer down!"

The picketing cops threw down their signs and ran to the alley.

"Can't we do anything?" Lewis wheezed as Robo's body continued to jerk.

Spotting a stack of discarded planks, Lewis shoved Stef away and, grabbing a wooden board, ran toward her partner. Wielding the plank like a baseball bat, she sent a blow smashing into Robo's chest.

RoboCop's arms left the transformer just as it exploded into flames. The force of the explosion sent Lewis tumbling backward. Robo flew across the alley, slamming into the wall opposite the transformer. He slowly slid down the wall, his body charred and smoking.

He did not move.

Lewis rushed over to him and extended a hand to touch his chest. Her skin sizzled. "Jesus!" she cried, yanking her burned fingers away.

"Get a stretcher!" she called. "Get him inside!"

Stef whirled around at the crowd of wide-eyed officers behind him. "You heard her!" he bellowed. "Move it!"

With seconds, there was no sign of any picket line in front of the station as all the police snapped to.

Four men raced out of the stationhouse, carrying a stretcher into the alley.

Robo's inert form continued to smolder.

The four men lowered the stretcher.

"He's too hot!" Stef cautioned. "Don't touch him. Use your jackets to lift him."

Lewis, Stef, and Whittaker doffed their jackets and wrapped them around Robo's legs. They slowly lifted the heavy metal limbs as the other cops slid the stretcher beneath him.

"Why the hell would he do something as stupid as that?" Stef asked Lewis.

Lewis was trying to keep from crying. "OCP gave him crazy commands. Screwed him up. Made him a bad cop. He fried himself to get rid of them."

"He couldn't wait to get back on the job," Whittaker said to Stef. "He knew how things were out in the streets and he wanted to go back."

Stef blinked. "What are you trying to tell me?"

"Just that Murphy *liked* doing his *job*. And he thought it needed *doing*."

Stef gazed down at Robo. "Shit, Murphy! You're one special kind of asshole." He turned to the other cops. "All right, we're gonna need a lot of help lifting this stretcher. Murphy weighs a ton."

A dozen cops ran to the stretcher, grabbing it in any way possible.

"One," Stef ordered, "two, *lift!*"

Amidst a chorus of curses and grunts, the stretcher slowly rose. The cops zigzagged their way toward the stationhouse's entrance, trampling their discarded picket signs.

Suddenly Robo's body began to thrash about.

"Shit!" Stef cried. "It's slipping!"

Robo's body gave a violent jerk, sending the cops tumbling and his body sliding onto the ground. Robo hit the pavement and slowly sat up.

He gazed up at the cops and clicked into command mode.

On his visor, superimposed above the faces of the curious policemen, Robo saw the command LIST DIRECTIVES.

After his computers ran a search, the words DIRECTIVES NOT FOUND appeared.

Robo slowly got to his feet and stood steadily. Calmly, he turned to Lewis. "How is your hand?"

"Stings a little," she said. "No big deal. How are you feeling?"

Robo formed a fist with his left hand. "Fed up."

He turned on the cops and began to walk away.

"What's bugging you, Murphy?" Whittaker asked.

"Cain," Robo said, halting and facing the cops. "Cain is bugging me."

"Who the hell is Cain?" Stef asked.

"You've spent too long on the picket line," Lewis said.

"Damn straight we have," Whittaker agreed.

"So, who's Cain?" Stef demanded a second time.

"Who do you think makes the NUKE?" Lewis asked.

Robo again began to walk toward his awaiting TurboCruiser.

Stef glanced at Lewis. "Shit, he just can't . . ."

Lewis shrugged.

Stef yelled at Robo's back. "You can't go after that fucker solo, Murphy! He'll rip you to pieces! Just like he did before."

"The hell he will," Whittaker said, walking toward a second TurboCruiser.

Robo continued his solitary march, trailed only by Whittaker. His mind was in turmoil as rage welled up from within him. He wanted revenge, true, but not just for the harm Cain had done to him.

He wanted to *fix* things somehow. He was a cop. A good cop. Children were being lost all around him. Children—the future—their young faces hardened, their systems brimming with poison. The future of the world depended on the children. They must be protected.

"Hey, Murphy," Whittaker called. "I'm going to tag along if it's okay with you."

"It's okay with me," Robo replied.

The other cops—who, moments before, had been picketing—all began to walk toward their long-parked cruisers.

"It's time we acted like cops again," one officer stated.

Stef stood there blinking. "Shit," he said, "this is crazy! The union's gonna crucify us. They got a list!"

But, he reasoned to himself, *I've always thought the union was run by a bunch of assholes.*

Stef jogged across the street. "Hey, Whittaker,

134

wait up! You ain't going nowhere without your partner!"

Whittaker slid behind the wheel of his TurboCruiser and turned the engine over. Stef slid into the shotgun seat. "Okay, Murphy," Stef muttered. "Let's get this goddamned show on the road!"

20

RoboCop and Lewis led the small parade of police cruisers through the streets of Old Detroit.

People began trotting out of their homes and businesses to see the sight up close.

"What the heck is that?" one hot-dog vendor asked a loitering cabbie.

"Cops!" the cabbie answered, amazed. "And they ain't holding no picket signs!"

"Way to go!" the vendor said, waving at the fleet of cruisers.

"Welcome back!" another man called.

"Go, Police!" an old bag lady yelled, raising her hand in a clutched fist of solidarity.

The police continued onward.

Miles ahead of them, in the River Rouge district, Cain and Angie pulled up in their limo, Catzo behind the wheel, before the large Tokugawa Brewery. A dozen of Cain's hoods along with Hob were already there, awaiting his arrival.

Angie looked up at the sleek building. "It's beautiful!" She smiled.

Cain reached into his jacket pocket and produced a deed. "It's ours. Bought and paid for. We're coming out of the shadows, dearie. We're going to stand tall in the sunlight for a change."

"I don't get it," Catzo muttered, following Cain, Angie, and Hob inside the building.

The interior of the brewery was vast, and were it not for the presence of several inches of dust, it would have looked like the set of a futuristic science-fiction film. Large metal vats sat side by side, and tubing was everywhere.

"Beer?" said Catzo. "I don't get it."

"We'll reduce the alcohol content"—Cain was grinning—"to demonstrate our commitment to public health."

"You're going to start this place up again?" the oaf called Catzo asked, his face a fleshy question mark.

"At full capacity." Cain chuckled.

"You're gonna make beer?" Catzo asked.

"We'll even rehire the old staff," Cain said. "Pay them well. We'll be a legitimate business. Beyond suspicion."

"But why do we want to make beer?" Catzo queried.

"Jesus!" Hob said, screwing up his small face into a mask of astonishment. "You are thick. It's a cover. It'll keep the cops looking the other way."

Catzo blinked, still not quite comprehending the Big Picture. Cain sighed. "Let's continue the tour."

He walked up to a large white-enamel door, the size of those found leading into a bank vault. Hob scampered forward and punched a twenty-digit code into an electronic combination lock. The door swung open without a sound.

"I think you'll understand now," Cain said, leading the trio inside.

Outside, meanwhile, the police cruisers had pulled onto the brewery grounds. The cops scrambled out, fully armed, and began trotting toward the large building.

"Now, isn't this something?" Cain asked Catzo, pointing out the well-crafted second brewery room.

Inside the second room stood two armored trucks, a 1950s antique airstream trailer, and a huge trailer truck, its back door open. Large barrels, connected by tubes leading into the trailer truck, sat unattended.

"This, my flock," Cain announced, "is the heart of our new enterprise."

Cain stood at the back of the truck, while Catzo lumbered up behind him. Inside the truck was a mountain of state-of-the-art lab equipment.

"NUKE!" Cain was beaming. "Made right here. Every one of its chemical components will be manufactured right here."

"Made in America," Angie added with a wink.

"We'll make that *mean* something again," said Cain patriotically, wrapping an arm around Catzo's broad shoulders.

"Phew!" Catzo grinned. "I'm really relieved. I thought for a minute there that we were just going to make beer."

"This is an awful lot of stuff," Angie said reverently, gazing at the equipment. "We can make shitloads of NUKE."

"Well put," Cain replied. "We're reaching out, city by city. It'll be like a revolution. Shared consciousness for all. Shared happiness."

"Plus," Hob pointed out to the blinking Catzo, "the unit price will plummet."

Catzo continued to blink.

"The more we make, the cheaper NUKE will get," Hob said, exasperated. "The *more* we'll sell."

"Great!" Catzo blurted out.

Hob tilted his head to the right side, toward the doors, straining his ears. "Shhhh!" he hissed.

"What?" Catzo asked.

"Shut up!" Hob replied. "I hear something."

Outside of Cain's inner sanctum, in the main brewery facility, the police were silently pouring in through the unlocked doors, their guns at the ready.

Robo was in the lead. He eyed the brewery equipment and, using his RoboVision, scanned the area.

Lewis walked alongside Robo, unaware that she was now directly in the crosshair scope of a high-powered rifle trained on her from the scaffolding above.

Lewis walked past a storage tank, out of the line of fire. Stef stepped up, taking Lewis's place.

Robo continued to analyze the situation. His eyes widened. He stepped forward and shoved Stef to the ground.

"Hey!" Stef exclaimed.

Robo launched his Auto-9 into his hand, raised the gun, and fired at the ceiling.

The shot took the hood above by surprise. The

bullet slammed into and through the rifle's scope and continued to sizzle into the man's right eye and, finally, his brain.

The man jerked backward and fell from the scaffolding with a high-pitched scream.

Stef scrambled to his feet while more and more hoods appeared, as if by magic, from within the bowels of the cavernous building.

"Fan out!" Stef yelled.

Inside the second brewery room, the sound of gunfire could now be heard. The quartet of gang-leaders froze.

Angie ran up to a window. "It's the *cops*!"

Catzo's face reddened. "We're not even *ready*! We don't have a *chance*!"

Cain walked over to the window and peered at the scene through a pair of small sunglasses. The area outside the brewery was in chaos. A running firefight was going on, with hoods and cops racing this way and that, firing wildly. His reed-thin body heaved a shoulder-raising sigh. "Stay calm," he cautioned, deadpanned. "We have the NUKE formula. We can set up operations anywhere. Catzo, get the teams into position and hold them off for as long as you can. This is what we've trained for."

Catzo hesitated. "I don't want to go back to prison. I'm really serious about that."

Cain patted Catzo on the back, leading the hulking man toward the combination door. "My friend, no prison will hold you. Not for long. We take care of our own. Now, into battle, Catzo!"

Catzo nodded like a punch-drunk fighter and jogged out of the room, his mini-Uzi drawn.

Cain turned to Angie and Hob. "Now let's get the hell out of here!"

In the main brewery room, Catzo rallied his troops. His minions regrouped and took up positions behind the heavy brewery equipment, their guns blazing.

The police, out of practice for weeks, had all they could do to stay out of the line of fire.

Stef and Whittaker crouched behind a vat. "Well," said Stef, "if nothin' else, the picketing has made our legs a lot stronger."

Whittaker nodded. "Might as well exercise 'em."

The two darted out from behind their cover and ran forward toward the hoods, bullets pinging the floor all around them. They fired into the maelstrom ahead of them, taking out three of the hoods, before coming to a rest behind the next vat. The cops behind them, seeing the tactic, began to leapfrog their way closer to the thugs as well.

The hoods were soon pinned down.

Stef pointed toward the ceiling. He raised his gun, took careful aim, and sent a small avalanche of electronic brewery equipment crashing down upon the hoods.

The hoods scattered. Most were nailed immediately by the blazing police guns.

"Secure the area and take it outside," Stef ordered, surveying the carnage before him.

He and Whittaker led the rest of the police outside the brewery, toward the loading dock.

Robo prowled the outside of the brewery, hardly noticing the gunfire around him. Cain was near. He could *feel* it.

In the back room of the brewery, Angie blasted the advancing police with a machine gun. Little Hob, his face a mask of intense concentration, sprayed volley after volley of mini-Uzi fire.

"If we can't kill them," Hob reasoned, "let's mess up their cars."

Hob's lips formed a thin smile as he began targeting the parked TurboCruisers.

Outside the building, RoboCop adjusted his hearing. He heard Hob's voice distinctly. Where the child was, Cain would be, he reasoned.

He marched toward the rear of the building, near the loading dock.

The rest of the police fanned out behind him.

Robo ambled onward. Suddenly he stiffened his body and cocked his head. A roar emerged from inside the building.

The roll-down metal loading door exploded, and two armored trucks burst forward from within the brewery, heading directly for Robo.

Angie gunned the accelerator of the first truck. It hit Robo dead-on, sending him tumbling under its wheels.

"Murphy!" called Lewis from the legion of police behind the fallen hero.

Riding shotgun in the first truck, Hob heaved a tear-gas canister out onto the loading area. The canister ignited upon impact, sending a thick, choking column of gas into the small army of police. Hob heaved another and another, and soon the police were caught in a man-made fog. They staggered, choking and wheezing, away from the area.

Robo slowly got to his feet as the second truck

roared by him. He ran a quick check on his systems. He was intact.

Another engine roared to life nearby. Using his thermovision to cut through the tear gas, he saw one of Cain's hoods sitting on a large Harley-Davidson and gunning the engine.

The hood made an attempt to zip away from the building and follow the two escape trucks.

"Not this time," Robo said as the Harley thundered forward.

Robo calculated at what point the Harley would pass near him and made sure he clanked his way to that point seconds before the cycle. Clenching his left hand in a fist, he raised it at the last possible second.

His fist smashed into the head of the passing cyclist, sending the thug tumbling backward onto the ground. Without thinking twice, Robo righted the fallen chopper and swung his large frame onto it. He revved the engine and sped away from the brewery.

The rest of the gathered law-enforcement officers watched RoboCop pursue the speeding trucks.

"He'll never catch them," Stef said, wiping the tears from his eyes. "The vans have too much of a head start."

"He'll catch them," Lewis said. "That's just the kind of guy he is."

"Come on," Whittaker said, motioning to the ruptured metal door of the back room. "Let's see if Cain has any other surprises for us."

Lewis, Stef, Whittaker, and a cop named Merkel walked gingerly into Cain's inner sanctum. The large trailer truck stood in the center of the room. The four cops padded to the rear of the truck. The vehicle's loading doors were open.

Stef motioned the others back. He sidled up to the rear doors and looked inside. His eyes widened. In the back of the truck, rigged to blow, was a wad of plastique.

"Get down!" he said, turning around. Stef threw himself to the floor just as the truck exploded. A vast fist of fire smashed through the walls and ceiling of the room, sending metal chunks slicing through space above the four prone cops.

Lewis choked on the smoke. The cop named Merkel crawled up to Stef and dragged his unconscious form away from the blazing inferno that had moments before been a big rig.

From out of nowhere, Catzo appeared. "Hey, Cop!"

Whittaker raised his head. Catzo's large left boot slammed into Whittaker's stomach, sending the officer rolling and groaning across the floor.

Lewis leaped to her feet behind Catzo. The big man whirled and, pulling a .45, fired a round at near point-blank range.

Catzo's shot echoed in the room. The slug slammed into Lewis's chest, hitting her flak jacket. The force of the impact knocked the wind out of her and sent her staggering backward. A weasel named Gillette, Catzo's right-hand man, leaped from the other side of the wall of flame and grabbed Lewis's arm, knocking down her pistol. He dragged the struggling cop headfirst toward the flaming truck.

Merkel, looking up from the inert Stef, raised his

revolver and fired two shots at Catzo. Catzo laughed as the bullets whizzed harmlessly by him. Taking out his own pistol, the thug ran forward and began pistol-whipping the stunned Merkel to the ground.

Catzo turned and relished his next shot. He'd blow that police bitch's head off.

Lewis was grappling with a determined Gillette, who was pushing her face closer and closer to the inferno. Lewis managed to execute a lethal kick, aiming for a spot directly between Gillette's legs. The punk moaned and released his grasp.

Catzo raised his gun to fire. Lewis, seeing the big man, pushed Gillette into the line of fire.

A surprised Catzo found himself pumping three slugs into his equally startled accomplice's torso, sending Gillette collapsing in a bloodied heap onto the brewery floor.

"Oh well," said Catzo philosophically. "At least you won't be hurt no more."

Catzo stared across the room. Lewis stood alone, her form illuminated by the blazing truck. Catzo chuckled. He raised his gun.

"Like shooting fish in a barrel." He squeezed the trigger. Click. Catzo stared at the gun in puzzlement. No more bullets? Damn. Oh, well. Catzo tossed down the .45 and produced two large knives out of his belt. He juggled them with the ease of a trained knife-fighter.

Lewis bent down and yanked a switchblade from her boot, swinging it open. "Just knives, then." She smiled.

Catzo danced toward Lewis, amazingly graceful

for his size. He swung his knife, toying with Lewis. The blade cut through her gunbelt and sent it clattering to the ground.

Catzo thrust and parried again, producing a razor-thin cut on a startled Lewis's right cheek.

"Just knives." Catzo giggled. "Never needed anything else. Not on girls."

Feeling as if he were already the victor, Catzo took a wild swing at Lewis. Lewis raised her right arm up, blocking Catzo's lunge. Crouching, she brought her left hand up hard. Her knife blade sliced into a spot on Catzo's chest between two ribs.

Catzo uttered a casual "Oh, shit."

Lewis slowly raised her body, twisting the blade as she did so. She felt the blade pierce Catzo's heart. She placed her face an inch from his and watched as the dumbfounded man died.

"Guess you haven't spent much time in Detroit, huh?" Lewis asked him.

Catzo stared at her, a blank look on his face. Lewis pulled her knife out of the man. His bulky body teetered for a moment before crashing onto the ground.

Lewis turned to Whittaker, still sprawled on the ground. He motioned to her that he was all right. She ran over to Stef and Merkel. They were pretty messed up but nowhere near death.

"Hey," Lewis called from the ruptured door to the cops outside, "call an ambulance! We have two men down in here."

21

The two trucks roared through the impoverished neighborhoods surrounding River Rouge. Angie and Hob smiled confidently at one another. "Cops are stupid," Angie concluded.

Hob nodded. "That's a given."

In the second truck, Cain gripped the wheel, feeling both angry and triumphant. He would see RoboCop dead for this little stunt. Millions of dollars wasted. Countless dreams put on hold. It wasn't right. America was supposed to be the land of opportunity. What was Cain's big crime? He was only trying to make a few bucks.

Cain's train of thought was derailed by the loud whine of an approaching engine.

He glanced over his shoulder nervously. Astride the Harley, RoboCop was gaining ground on the cumbersome armored truck.

Cain gunned the accelerator, but to no avail. The cycle continued to pull closer and closer. Soon Robo was at the driver's side of the truck, slowly overtaking it.

Cain cursed under his breath. He swerved the truck to the left, trying to pancake Robo against a long-abandoned tenement. Having expected the move, Robo revved the Harley and pulled ahead of the truck.

Cain let out a shriek of anger as the truck hopped the curb and slammed into the front of the tenement, neatly shearing off its front stoop. Cain wrestled the wheel, sending the truck careening back onto the road.

He glanced this way and that. There was no sign of either Robo or the cycle. Cain smiled confidently. "Squashed him like a bug!" He sighed happily.

Cain sent the truck speeding into a populated area of Old Detroit.

Three blocks ahead of the truck, Robo executed a screaming U-turn and sent the cycle speeding into oncoming traffic. Slaloming expertly through the screeching autos in his path, Robo zipped down an alley, turned on a forty-five-degree angle, and plunged down a street. At the far end of the block, Cain's truck appeared.

Behind the wheel of the truck, Cain suppressed a gasp as he spotted the metallic upholder of the law speeding directly toward him. No doubt about it: They were on a collision course.

"Okay, bucket brain," Cain said, stomping on the gas pedal. "It's time you experienced *real* pain." Cain's truck sped toward Robo.

Robo gritted his teeth and continued to sail onward. This was for the children, he told himself. For the future. He wrenched the throttle, picking up speed.

Cain laughed to himself. This was going to be too easy.

The Harley slammed into the front of the truck, sending Robo's body tumbling through space. The Harley was completely crushed by the front of the armored vehicle. Cain cackled. Then he lost his sense of humor.

Robo's airborne body crashed through the truck's windshield, smacking into Cain's screeching form full force. Metal met flesh. There was no contest.

The truck, dragging the Harley on its undercarriage, moaned forward, sending up a spray of sparks as metal sliced concrete. It zigzagged for a hundred yards before it groaned and flipped over onto its side.

The truck hit the pavement with a resounding crunch, its back doors wrenching open. A cloud of cash billowed into the air—millions of dollars in small bills. The startled residents of the impoverished neighborhood stopped in their tracks.

"Sonofabitch!" one wino declared, plucking a twenty-dollar bill out of the air. "It's raining money!"

Inside the cab of the truck, there was a sudden movement. A metal hand ripped the driver's door open, and RoboCop emerged.

He ignored the street people scrambling after the money and pushed onward.

There is going to be a lot of paperwork involved in this collar, he thought.

22

The Old Man, Johnson, and Dr. Faxx sat in the despot's penthouse office in silence. Dr. Faxx, sitting as primly as an ice sculpture, rested her hand on the Old Man's reassuringly. Johnson pretended not to notice.

Before them, a TV set was droning. A commercial. A beautiful woman wearing a string bikini stood before a full-length mirror that reflected a bright sun. The words "LOS ANGELES" appeared over her curves as an announcer intoned: "They say twenty seconds in the California sunshine is too much these days, ever since we lost the ozone layer."

The woman smiled and reached for a jar. She began to daub a black, tarlike substance across her breasts. "But that was before *Sun Block 5,000*," the omniscient announcer declared. "Just apply a pint to your body and . . ."

The bikini-clad tar baby stretched near a pool. ". . . you're good for *hours*. See you by the *pool!*"

The commercial ended, and newscasters Jess

Perkins and Casey Wong returned. Both still wore their smiles.

The Old Man stiffened somewhat as a video of RoboCop surrounded by cheerful cops hit the screen. "The police strike is over!" Jess declared. "And have they been busy! Led by RoboCop, Detroit police smashed the NUKE operation and apprehended the mysterious kingpin of the NUKE gang, who is rumored to be hovering between life and death at OCP's medical center."

A jittery video of Mayor Kuzak trying to choke Johnson in the middle of a crowded courtroom then appeared. Johnson rubbed the bruises on his neck.

"In other local news," Jess continued, "Mayor Cyril Kuzak was held in contempt for an outburst following his latest failure to block OmniConsumer-Products's hostile takeover of the city's government. OCP director of operations Donald Johnson had this to say."

The screen cut to Johnson, speaking in a hoarse whisper, addressing reporters: "The fact is that OCP can't foot the bill for an incompetent administration. We can, however, do much for this city once Mayor Kuzak and the people who got us into this mess are out of the way."

"Well said," commented the Old Man, flicking off the TV as a commercial featuring a Yuppie blowing his head off after ordering the wrong business phone system flickered onto the tube.

"Thank you, sir." Johnson smiled. "Nothing in our agenda has changed."

"Something *has* changed," the Old Man declared. "I don't like having the police back to work."

"That could turn out to be a plus for us, sir," said Dr. Faxx, smiling.

Johnson winced. The Old Man was in her power. He knew it.

"With the police back to work, the public will perceive us as a fair-minded corporation," Faxx stated.

"But we *are* a fair-minded corporation," said the Old Man. "All I'm trying to do is trim the fat from America. Restore it to its vitality!"

"But not everyone is as much of a visionary as you, sir." She smiled again.

"That's the problem with this country today," the Old Man began.

Johnson settled back into his chair. He was going to hear The Speech, again. Faxx was smiling at the Old Man like an adoring supplicant. Something about her smile gave Johnson the creeps.

23

A lone armored car sat outside the parking lot adjacent to the OCP medical center. In the front seat, Angie handed a pair of binoculars to Hob. "Third floor," she whispered. "Fourth from the left."

Hob raised the glasses nervously.

"That's where he is," Angie said. "See? They still got the light on."

"So what?" Hob retorted. "We shouldn't have come here, Angie. Somebody'll spot us."

"'We take care of our own,'" she whispered. "That's what he said."

"He said lots of things," Hob answered, handing back the binoculars. "Come on. Let's get out of here."

"He'll *kill* us if we don't come for him," Angie pointed out.

Hob leaned his head forward, as if to nap. "He's not killing anybody! You heard the news! Shit! He's probably dead by now anyway."

Angie's lower lip trembled. "Yeah, but . . . I don't know."

Hob turned toward her, his young face growing rigid and determined. There was a fire in his eyes now, a fire that Angie had only seen in the eyes of Cain. "You do what I say from now on! Start the motor and drive."

Angie nodded silently, responding to the new-found power in Hob's voice. She guided the armored truck away from the scene.

As they left, other lights on the third floor of the medical center flickered off. Cain's, however, remained well lit.

Inside his room, Cain was sprawled inert within a web of life-support equipment. He was conscious, his eyes staring widely at the glistening, gleaming machines all around him. Funny, he thought to himself. A machine had done this to him, and now machines were helping him. An artificial lung wheezed steadily to his right. A monitor tracked his heartbeat to the left. He heard the door to his room open. He turned his eyes toward the door.

Dr. Faxx walked in, a beatific smile on her face.

She glanced cautiously over her shoulder, making sure no one else on the floor had seen her. She entered the room, easing the door closed behind her. She locked it and walked to the bed, still smiling like an angel.

"Aren't you the mess," she cooed. "But I've got good news for you: You're going to get your chance."

Cain stared at her suspiciously. He tried to talk but was incapable of speech.

Faxx continued to smile. "Your chance to touch the eternal!"

Cain blinked.

Faxx produced a cellular phone from her purse and punched a few buttons. She raised the phone to her well-rounded lips. "Dr. Weltman? I'm afraid our patient has failed. . . . Yes, I'm quite certain. Please prepare a death certificate and scramble a surgical team. We only have six minutes before the tissue will be useless."

Cain glared at the woman. She was insane! He tried to thrash in his bed but discovered that he was tied down securely. Faxx tucked him in and placed a maternal kiss on his sweaty forehead. "Now," she whispered, "be a good little boy and get some rest."

Dr. Faxx tenderly disconnected the plug from Cain's artificial lung. Cain's eyes widened as he felt his insides collapse. He began to gurgle. His body convulsed, and his head felt as if it would explode. Cain wrenched a hand free of the tubing and wires and attempted to clutch at Dr. Faxx's blouse. Faxx didn't bother avoiding the move. She watched the hand as it paused, twitched, then fell back onto the bed.

Within seconds, Cain's cardiogram was as flat as a slice of Kansas highway.

Dr. Faxx tenderly placed Cain's hand back into a comfortable position. Facing a mirror, she adjusted her blouse and her hair. Then, walking to the door, she unlocked it.

Several interns rushed in with a stretcher. In an operating room minutes later, a surgical team scrambled around Cain's inert form. Faxx watched contentedly from a viewing stand above. The lead surgeon, Dr. Weltman, had never performed this complicated an operation before and was aware of the corporate pressure on him to not only perform it well but perform it perfectly.

"Switch blood to serum pumps," he instructed a masked nurse.

"Switch complete," the nurse replied.

Cain's lifeless eyes gaped at the lights above him.

"Give me current," Dr. Weltman ordered.

A second nurse turned on a console, and there was a sudden surge of electricity. Cain's body twisted spastically.

Weltman grabbed a scalpel and bent over Cain's head. "All right, I'm isolating the medulla. . . ."

Faxx watched with glee as the procedure went on. Cain's optical nerves and eyeballs, along with the brain and the spinal nervous system, were carefully removed and placed into a large, fluid-filled, glass tank. Life-support systems were hooked up to the tank.

After two hours, Dr. Weltman looked up at Faxx and nodded. He removed his mask and smiled at her. Faxx rushed down into the operating theater.

"Success?" she asked.

"Success," Weltman nodded.

An intern walked up to Weltman. "What should we do with that?"

He pointed to Cain's head, lying sans body on the operating table. Its eyes were gone, its cranium was empty. Weltman shrugged. "Toss it."

The intern picked up the remnants of the head and dumped it into a container. He wheeled the container out of the room.

Faxx smiled at the doctor. "Up for a drink, Doctor?"

"Of course, Doctor," Weltman replied.

The two doctors, accompanied by the assisting team, left the operating room.

Behind, in the tank, a pair of baleful eyes watched them go, their brain registering anger.

The essence of Cain—his mind, his memories, and his vision—made out the figures of Faxx and Weltman from behind the veil of thick fluid percolating around it.

Cain was alive.

Alive!

24

With the strike over, life returned to normal in the Old Detroit stationhouse, which is to say that hell was breaking loose every 6.7 seconds. In an office area housing dozens of cubicles, separated only by paper-thin pressboard "walls," cops sat bleary-eyed, taking complaints from agitated citizens. Lewis sat at a computer console, clumsily transcribing handwritten notes to CompuFiles. Robo-Cop walked by her.

"Hey, Murphy? That liquor store holdup last week—did you get the address?"

Robo didn't break step. "663 North Mitsubishi."

"Oh, right," Lewis said, continuing to mangle a keypad. "They had a hostage. What's that make the charge code?"

"Baker Allen Three, subsection twelve."

"Thanks." Lewis hit the wrong keys. "Shit."

Stef walked up to Robo. "Hey, Murphy, the sarge wants to see you in his office."

Robo nodded and walked toward Reed's office without saying a word.

Lewis glanced at Stef. "What's up?"

"Who the hell knows? Reed says it's *personal*. You tell me what that means." Stef shrugged, sliding into his own cubicle. "I hate paperwork."

Robo walked by a long stretch of actual office space, sputtering to a skidding halt as he heard a familiar voice. A female voice. The voice of Ellen Murphy, wife of Alex J. Murphy, deceased.

"That's all right, Tom," the voice announced. "I know where it is. I'll get it myself."

Ellen Murphy strode out of the office, empty coffee cup in hand, and walked directly into Robo. She stared up into Robo's deep blue eyes. Robo stood immobile. It was the closest thing to heartbreak he had experienced since breathing his last breath as a human.

"Uh, excuse me," he said politely.

Ellen's attorney, Tom Delaney, ran up behind Ellen. He shook his head, frowning.

Robo swiveled his head as another lawyer, a by-the-books type with a forehead filled with sweat, hopped onto the scene. "Oh, damnit!" Holzgang, the OCP attorney, muttered.

Delaney turned to Holzgang. "You said she wouldn't have to see him!"

Holzgang spun round and faced Reed's desk. Reed was already drumming his fingers on his desktop in exasperation. "Come on, Ellen."

Reed stood up and guided a white-faced Ellen away. Her eyes continued to gaze into Robo's as Reed led her down the corridor into a second office. Delaney faced RoboCop, pointing to the office. "My name is Tom Delaney," he announced. "I'm an attorney. My client is the widow of police officer Alex Murphy. I have to speak with you. It's very important."

Delaney guided Robo inside. An angry Holzgang followed. "I'm representing you from OCP, Robo-Cop. Don't say anything. Not one word!"

Delaney eased himself into a chair. Robo and Holzgang remained standing. "Have you been spying on Mrs. Murphy?" Delaney asked Robo.

The cyborg stared down at him in silence.

"Her neighbors have seen you drive by her home a dozen times in the past two months," Delaney continued.

Robo nodded. "Yes. I have."

Holzgang spun on the towering figure. "Will you *shut up!*"

Robo pivoted his body and stared down at the little man, his eyes blazing from beneath his visor. Holzgang's legs began to quiver as Robo said, hotly and evenly, "No . . . I will *not* shut up!"

Delaney, the younger of the two lawyers, was enjoying the scene. "I'd be the last man on earth to ever come between a man and his wife, but—"

Holzgang shook with rage. "This is *not* Alex Murphy," he said, thrusting a finger at Robo's metallic torso. "This is an OCP product that incorporates certain neurological matter from Murphy's corpse. And yes, Murphy signed a release for the parts before his death."

Holzgang glared at RoboCop. "And that's what *you're* going to say. On *tape!* So this doesn't happen again."

Robo ignored the frustrated Holzgang and listened to Delaney. "We're worried about her pension benefits. You see, OCP has been making threats."

Robo whirled and glared at Holzgang. The lawyer held his ground. "We want a statement from you. You cooperate, and Murphy's wife and kid get all the benefits of being the family of a shot cop. You mess with us, they get zip. Nada. Goose eggs."

Robo snarled and took a step toward the lawyer, catching himself in time and curbing his mounting anger. Delaney got to his feet. "Please, Officer," he said soothingly, "it's better for everyone involved if you cooperate. It's better for her. It's better for your son."

But what about me? Robo thought. "I will . . . cooperate," he announced.

Holzgang dismissed Delaney with a nod. The lawyer representing Murphy's wife disappeared, and a video cameraman took his place.

Outside, in the hallway, Lewis was making her way down the corridor, stacks of forms in her hands. She saw Robo standing next to the two men.

"All right," Holzgang said, "let's get this over with. Are you ready?"

Robo nodded. "I am ready."

Lewis peered into the office as Holzgang nodded to the video technician. The cameraman began the tape as Holzgang interviewed Robo. "If I were to describe you as a piece of machinery that utilized some living tissue, would that be accurate?"

"Yes," Robo answered.

"And so," said Holzgang with a smile, "you are not a human, are you?"

"I am not human," Robo announced.

"Therefore," Holzgang continued, "will you admit that you are not deserving of any rights accorded to human beings under the law?"

Robo locked his jaw and remained silent.

"I require an answer," Holzgang said.

Robo remained silent.

Holzgang turned to the cameraman. "Stop tape, John."

He faced Robo. "Look, I don't think you like me very much. You probably think I'm a real bastard. But you've got me wrong—all wrong."

Robo turned to leave the room, Holzgang at his heels. "*You're* the one who's being the bastard," Holzgang argued. "Do you have any idea what you're doing to that poor woman?"

Robo turned to face the lawyer. Holzgang yanked a folder out of his briefcase nearby and thrust it into Robo's hands. "Take a look at her file." Holzgang sneered. "Go on, *read it!*"

Robo scanned the file as Holzgang continued to harangue him. "Up until a few months ago, Mrs. Murphy wouldn't leave her bedroom. She even began to wear her husband's clothes, just to feel closer to him. Then there were the therapists and the hypnotists and the harmonic treatments. She's barely started to accept the loss. She's gone back to work. Then *you* pull this shit!"

Robo's hands began to tremble. Holzgang closed in for the kill. "You're ripping her to pieces, you know that? And for *what*? What can *you* offer her? Companionship? Love? A man's love? You think you've got what it takes to be a *husband* to her?"

Robo gently closed the folder and handed it back

to Holzgang. "No," he said quietly. He nodded to the cameraman. "You may proceed with your taping."

Holzgang started up again. "Do you believe you are in any way entitled to the rights and privileges accorded to human beings under our system of law?"

"No." Robo sighed. "I have no rights."

"You are simply a machine?"

"I am . . . a machine."

"Nothing more?"

"Nothing more," Robo said flatly.

"That'll do it," said Holzgang, and the cameraman lowered the video unit. "You may come with me now."

Lewis darted into an empty work space as Holzgang led Robo into the office where an ashen-faced Ellen sat. Delaney was beside her.

"Alex!" Ellen exclaimed, starting out of her chair.

Robo stood silently, as motionless as a statue.

"Don't you know me, Alex?" Ellen began to sob.

Robo regarded her stonily.

"Don't you recognize me?" Ellen asked.

Holzgang nudged Robo. "Answer the lady."

Robo's words were slow in coming. Ellen left her seat and placed her hand on Robo's chest, where Alex J. Murphy's heart would have been had there still been an Alex J. Murphy.

"Alex," she sobbed, "it doesn't matter what they've done to you. . . . It doesn't. It doesn't!"

Robo stared at the wall on the opposite side of the room, avoiding her gaze. "I am sorry, ma'am," he announced. "I do not know you."

Robo turned and marched out of the room. Ellen

collapsed into her chair in tears, overwhelmed by the loss of her husband a second time.

Delaney gingerly supported the woman and led her through and out of the stationhouse, where a cab awaited them.

Robo stood alone in an empty office and, through a shattered window, watched them go.

25

RoboCop sat motionless on his throne in the Robo-Chamber, his helmet off. Tak Akita had given up trying to monitor Robo's system readouts: There were none. He left the room, muttering dark oaths.

Robo continued to sit. Lewis appeared at the doorway, carrying her brown-bagged lunch with her. "Mind if I have my lunch here?"

Robo stared blankly ahead.

Lewis shrugged, sat down across from Robo, and pulled a sandwich out of her bag.

"You know what really pisses me off?" she said, munching on her dripping sandwich. "The shit that son of a bitch pulled. Extortion is what it was. They don't even *pay* you for the work you do."

Robo's left hand began tapping up and down on the metal armrest, a move Lewis recognized as totally human, a gesture of contained fury.

"I know you had to say that stuff," Lewis continued. "But it's just not true. It's not like they say. You're not what they say you are. You're not a machine. You're more than that."

Lewis gazed deeply into Robo's eyes. "You're a whole lot more than that."

Robo's hand closed around the armrest, crumpling the metal. Without a word, he stood up, grabbed his helmet, and stormed out of the room. Lewis threw down her sandwich. "Yeah, nice talking with you, too."

She trotted after Robo. She heard his TurboCruiser screech onto the street in front of the station. "Damn," she muttered.

Minutes later, Robo's car skidded to a stop outside a vast junkyard, a chainlink fence firmly in place to keep the public out of the refuse-littered landscape.

Robo marched out of his car and approached the fence. He grabbed it with his left hand and, with a sudden jerk, ripped the fence apart. He walked into the junkyard, easing the fragmented fence closed behind him.

Robo walked silently through the burial ground of mangled cars and discarded home appliances. Cranes swung back and forth, lifting the metal debris with their powerful magnets. Robo watched as the cranes sucked up the forgotten metal slabs and loaded them onto a large rolling conveyor belt. The conveyor belt fed metallic debris into a screeching, screaming, flailing machine that spat out bits of shrapnel when it was done munching the junk.

Robo scanned the junkyard.

He gazed down at his own hands.

Metal.

For a moment, it appeared to him that they were also rusted, discarded, without purpose.

He closed his eyes and daydreamed, seeing himself frozen solid by rust. He envisioned the mighty magnets lifting his long-outmoded, creaky, corroded body toward the conveyor belt. The conveyor accepted the offering without question. The whining, flailing machine nourished itself on Robo's body, tearing it to pieces with rotating, razor-sharp teeth. His remains exited the belly of the beast on the far side of the conveyor. Robo's remains landed with those of the toasters, the microwaves, the VW vans.

"Hey!" came a voice.

Robo blinked. Lewis was scrambling through the junkyard. He turned his back on her and continued staring at the conveyor belt.

Lewis's anger built as she approached the solitary soldier. Reaching down, she picked up a large length of pipe and stalked toward Robo, livid.

"Murphy!" she yelled. "What the *hell* do you think you're doing out here! Damn it, you answer me!"

Robo kept his back to her.

"I said, *answer me!*" Lewis screamed. She stopped four feet behind him, aware that his gaze was focused on the ever-hungry conveyor belt.

"Feeling pretty damned *sorry* for yourself, aren't you?" she sneered. "I said *answer me*, goddamnit!"

She leaped forward and swung the pipe at Robo. Clang! She made contact with his back. No movement. No reaction.

"I am *so* sick of your *shit!*" she screamed.

She hit him a second time. Robo slowly turned and faced her, staring at her impassively.

Lewis's face was beet red now. "You're not *fooling* me like you are everybody else! I *know* you! I know *what* you are! I know *who* you are!"

Furious at Robo's passive manner, she swung the pipe again. Robo lifted his right hand and caught it, wrenched it from her grasp, and tossed it away. In a total rage, she tried to tackle him, punching him in the chest. Robo watched her as she let out a yelp of pain, pulling her fist away from his torso.

"Are you in need of medical attention?" he asked mechanically.

"Oh, fuck you," Lewis said, wincing. "'Are you in need of medical attention?' Jeezuz, you don't even know how to talk to a woman. Thè hell with you. You like that machine over there? You want that machine? Go to it, buster. Go Cuisinart yourself."

Lewis turned to leave. Robo extended his arm and pulled her close to him. She tilted her head up, surprised. Their faces were so close they could kiss. She gazed at him, trying to both play it tough and crumble in his embrace.

"Do you have something to say to me?" she asked.

"Yes." Robo nodded.

He abruptly released her. She took a step backward, her eyes remaining on his.

Robo titled his head like a good toy soldier. "Thank you for your concern," he announced.

He began to march away. He passed a confused Lewis and made his way to his cruiser. He got into his vehicle and drove off, leaving Lewis still standing in the junkyard.

She sighed and began to walk to her vehicle, gingerly stepping over the mounds of trash.

"Men!" she cursed.

26

Hob curled his skinny elfin body in a large chair and watched the tube, hogging down a plate of greasy french fries oozing catsup. He was child old before his time, with a megalomaniac's brain thriving behind his eyes. He wolfed down the fries in a feeding frenzy, enjoying his newfound sense of power, of *purpose*. Behind him, lounging on a couch, the frizzy-haired Angie sipped champagne. She was feeling younger, more alive, than she had in years. Well, maybe months. Her brain was so clouded for the most part that all sense of time had become totally relative.

Hob gazed at the TV. "Hey," he said. "I'm a kid, and this strikes me as being dumb."

Angie nodded. She relished guiding Hob through puberty.

On the tube, a contortionist violinist was finishing an excruciating version of the golden oldie "Born to Be Wild" on a stage constructed in a slipshod manner in front of a bank of telephones. Bored operators stared at the phones, none of which were ringing. A banner behind the stage read "SAVE OUR CITY TELETHON." As the violinist wrenched out the last gut-wrenching note, an overly enthusiastic Mayor Kuzak hopped onto the stage, slapping his palms together as if trying to ward off frostbite.

"Spike Stretzletski from Linden, New Jersey, folks," Kuzak boomed. "A transplanted Detroiter, he came out for Detroit. Now you come out for him! The lines are open, waiting for your pledge! Whatever you can spare. Let's keep this grand city afloat, huh?"

A single phone rang in the background. A bored, gum-popping operator made a move to answer it. Kuzak leaped at the phone, yanking it to his ear.

"Hi, howareya," Kuzak bubbled. "It's the mayor."

The voice of an old woman creaked over the phone. "I've lived in Detroit City all my life, so I'm sending in one dollar right now."

Kuzak's smile froze. "Yes, ma'am. Thank you, ma'am."

He faced the pledge board. "So, where does that put us, Gilly?"

An overaged showgirl, whose torso defied several laws of gravity every time she took a step, waddled up to the electronic scorecard. "MOTOWN NEEDS: $37,985,300.00." The board whirled. "RECEIVED SO FAR: $4,800.75."

Kuzak clutched to his smile like a drowning sailor to a life preserver.

In his new penthouse, Hob turned to Angie. He grinned, hatching a scheme. He leaned over Angie's ample breasts and whispered something in her ear.

She eagerly agreed and punched a number into her phone. Hob watched with glee as Mayor Kuzak spun around as another phone resounded.

Kuzak picked up the phone. "It never rains . . . it pours!"

Angie breathed heavily into the phone. "Mr. Mayor?"

"Yes, this is Mr. Mayor," said Kuzak, beaming. "Please turn down your set."

Hob lowered the volume on the TV as Angie, apparently asthmatic, hissed into the phone. "Your Honor. This is your lucky day."

Hob began to cackle as the mayor's eyes lit up. *This* would teach OCP to fuck around with Hob and his kind.

Half an hour later, at OCP headquarters, things were falling apart quite rapidly.

Johnson trotted to the elevator as Councilman Poulos, summoned by the Old Man, got off on the penthouse level, obviously disoriented. Johnson pumped his hand. "This way, Councilman. Take a look at what OCP has to offer."

Johnson yanked Poulos toward a display of robotic weaponry.

Poulos was confused, to say the least, as Johnson pointed to one perk after another. "You know, Mr. Johnson, I really don't feel I have a future at City Hall."

"Nobody does," said Johnson happily. "But you've got a sweet desk job waiting at OCP, my friend. That's if your information is worth my time."

Poulos blinked. "It is. The mayor might have

found a way to beat the foreclosure. He thinks he's found a benefactor. Someone who will bail the city out."

"What?" Johnson gulped. "Some other corporation?"

"Not as far as I know," Poulos said. "But definitely big business. A big wheeler-dealer."

Johnson swallowed the phlegm that was rapidly gurgling its way up to his throat. He led Poulos on a tour of the opulent facility and continued to stroke him. Shit, he thought, if Detroit got away from the Old Man, it was Johnson's ass on the griddle.

He gazed at the ceilings above him. Sometimes he wondered if he should've become a priest, like his mama wanted.

PART THREE

"Maybe this world is another planet's
Hell."

—Aldous Huxley

27

Dr. Faxx stood anxiously by as wild encephalogram signals spiraled across a monitor perched upon a horizontal metal form. Sweating, robotics whiz Schenck gaped at it. "I'd have to review the interfacing again," he said nervously. "There's something here that I didn't expect. This brain has a chemical dependency."

"Exactly why I chose it." Faxx smiled demurely. "Turn it on."

Schenck hesitated.

"Turn it on!" Faxx demanded.

Schenck nodded dumbly and pressed a button on a large console.

The blackness of the monitor's screen snapped to. A ghostly white oval shape appeared. Gradually the shape swirled into a facial form: a computer-generated deathmask of Cain. Slowly, its eyes opened. The eyes focused and looked around. Within the great bestial form lying before them, within its bowels of computer-generated hardware, a soul awakened, and first felt the pain of being locked into an enternal hell. The face opened its mouth and emitted a silent scream.

"Such terrible pain," Faxx noted. "Now you'll see the benefits of choosing an addictive personality."

Faxx's hands slid across the touchpads on a small handheld command module.

From the belly of the creature lying before them on a massive table, a feeding mechanism popped up.

Faxx smiled and slide a NUKE canister into the mechanism. The mechanism snatched it and plunged it into the creature's inner organs. The sound of pumping echoed throughout the room.

Faxx's hands slid over the control module once again. She extended her hand toward the stomach of the cyborg and slid the drained canister out. "There now. That's enough. Feeling better?"

On the monitor, Cain's holographic face went placid and tranquil, NUKEd out of its gourd.

"You see, Mr. Schenck? A little NUKE and he's no trouble at all."

The two leaped back as—slam!—two metal plates closed above the monitor. It was now nothing more than a featureless robotic face on top of the nine-foot body of a titanic metallic form.

"Tell them we're ready for the demonstration," Faxx said to Schenck.

She gazed adoringly upon the latest leap forward into robotics. On the slab before her was the ideal combination of cyborg science, topped by the totally subservient addictive personality of the thug named Cain.

"They're going to love this," Faxx said, envisioning her own promotion.

The metallic monster that was once Cain waited until the two scientists had left the room. He slowly rose from the table and teetered to his feet, snapping open the two metal plates that encased the black computer-generated face. He forced his soul to come to. The blurred white face of Cain, the human, gradually formed on the visage.

He gazed down at his newfound black and sleek metallic gray body. Nine feet tall it was. A metallic X on the mighty torso opened up to reveal a feeding tube. NUKE time. That was certainly all right. "Danger" and "Nuclear Energy: Keep Out" decals littered his front.

He glanced to his left and right. He had two powerful, three-pronged crablike arms. There were four spotlights—one on the top of each shoulder and two attached just below each armpit—and a smaller light he could see on his back, his head now having the ability to rotate 360 degrees. Yes, he could target any prey with these pretty little suckers.

His left arm was basically topped by a club, and atop the club was a 7.9mm rotary cannon—a Gatling gun. An ammunition shuttle ran below his chest. Quite a powerful guy, this newly made Cain.

Cain continued to *sense* his left arm. If he didn't want to beat something to death, he could eject the club and extend a 22-foot solid tube that would effectively grasp an enemy as if he were a fish and reel him in for the kill.

He turned to his back. Behind his right shoulder blade was placed a 20mm pom-pom gun—a two-barrel cannon. He flexed his back. The cannon slid up and over his shoulder, aiming at the wall in front of him. Nice touch, Cain thought.

Also on his back was a welded shield that could rise and fan out to become an effective bullet-proofing device. He liked that. He liked that a lot.

Cain was delirious as the NUKE pulsated through his system. Cain flexed his mighty legs. He walked across the lab, wobbling slightly. He noted that his feet had disc brakes and shock absorbers. Each foot had two dual-grasping claws, curled up next to his ankles: crustacean toes, capable of grasping anything should he topple, or crushing anyone near him should they fall.

Cain instinctively felt the presence of hydraulic pumps. He took what, for a human, would be a deep breath and found his torso rising almost one foot. He took another deep breath and found his shut-tered head rising another foot. Hell, at full tilt, he could stand eleven feet tall.

He twisted his torso around. It spun in a full circle.

He flexed his chest.

Small explosive hatches popped open, able to launch minimissiles at whatever threatened him. The computer-generated face of Cain smiled, high atop the monitor housed in his metallic head's shell.

They shouldn't have done this to him, he realized.

He would never touch the eternal—not like this.

But he was determined to touch a lot of people.

Cain's holographic face sneered. He was no longer part of the program. Sorry about that.

Across town, Mayor Kuzak's limo rolled across a strip of long-disused railroad tracks and rumbled to a halt outside a rickety gate. In the back seat of the limo, the smiling mayor, a worried Poulos, and an even more worried elderly attorney named Darren Thomas, sat. The driver in the front seat of the limo wasn't too thrilled about the meeting spot either.

Kuzak leaned forward toward the driver, Corman. "You sure this is the place?"

Corman nodded. "You said three lefts off the Toyota-Ford E-Way. If you got it right, we're at the right place."

"Of course I got it right." Kuzak grinned. "I wrote it down."

The mayor's eyes bulged as a tall, well-dressed and well-scarred man appeared at the gate, who motioned him forward into a factory complex.

"Follow the man, Corman," Kuzak said.

The driver grunted and sent the limo purring after the ambling man. "I don't know about this," Poulos muttered. "Damned strange place to meet an *investor*."

"Don't be so judgmental," said the mayor. "He has a nice suit and a nice haircut."

The limo hit a dirt hole and got stuck. The driver gunned the engine, causing the rear wheels to spew an arc of mud and grit in the car's wake.

"I don't like this," Poulos whispered. "Let's get out of here while we can!"

"I know what I'm doing," Kuzak assured him, climbing out of the earthbound limo. "Come on, let's go."

Kuzak led Thomas and Poulos through an opened door at the factory complex. Inside the factory, they were greeted by an equally well-dressed and equally ugly hood.

"If you've got any cash on you, now's the time to put it in a sock and hand it over," grumbled Poulos.

"That's just plain rude," Kuzak said, extending a hand and winking at the new hood. "Howya doin'," he enthused. "I bet you all have great plans for this place. Golly, lots of potential hereabouts."

Without returning the burst of enthusiasm, the hood silently turned and led the terrified trio further inside.

A single light blazed at the far side of the hangar-sized room. The trio followed the hood toward the source of illumination. A small conference table had been placed below a low-hanging light. Four hoods stood nearby. At the table, an accountant-type fingered the pads on his laptop computer as tiny Hob whispered information into his left ear. At another end of the table, Angie, exposing her legs as much as possible without causing a vice raid, polished her nails.

The mayor's party approached the table.

Hob nodded to the accountant, and the man disappeared into the darkness.

Kuzak ambled toward the table. "I wonder if any of you can help me. I'm looking for a Mr. Hob."

Angie slithered out of her chair and stood behind the boy, her breasts resting upon his head. She pointed at the lad.

Hob nodded at the mayor. "Sit down, Mr.

Mayor," he chirped. He turned to one of the hoods. "Get us some Cokes."

Kuzak sat down before Hob, who asked, "How much do you need? Money, I mean?"

The mayor giggled nervously. "Well, our current debt to OCP is . . ."

Councilman Poulos sat down beside the mayor. "Thirty-seven million, four hundred and eighty thousand, nine hundred and eleven dollars."

Hob shrugged. "Thirty-seven million, four hundred and eighty thousand, nine hundred and eleven dollars. Guess you're in pretty deep shit."

"We need all the help we can get, young man." Kuzak grinned lamely.

"Tell you what," Hob offered. "Put me down for fifty. Just to make sure."

"Fifty thousand?" asked the mayor, beaming.

"Don't be a queer," replied Hob. "Fifty million."

"Oh, goddamnit," Poulos moaned. "Let's get out of here."

Poulos got to his feet and turned to leave. Kuzak hesitated, then got to his feet as well. "Jeez, the things people will do just to get a chance to meet me."

Kuzak found a small Beretta placed firmly against his crotch by a well-dressed hood.

Hob faced the darkness to his left. "Show the man."

A well-armored truck backed into the light, and four niftily suited thugs swung open its back doors. Hundreds of millions of dollars were stacked to the ceiling.

The mayor's jaw dropped, nearly rebounding off his

shaking knees. "That . . . tha . . . tha . . . mo . . . mon . . . money . . . moneymoneymoney."

"So." Hob shrugged. "Will fifty cover it?"

Kuzak nodded. "Yeah. YEAH! That'd do it."

He glanced at his stunned compatriots. "Don't you think that would do it, men?"

He turned again to Hob. "Yeah, that *definitely* would do it, Mr. Hob."

Hob chuckled, sounding like a chipmunk. "Okay. So, now we know how to fix your problems. Let's talk about mine."

The old lawyer, Thomas, pulled Kuzak aside. "Please excuse us for a moment." He smiled at Hob before facing Kuzak. "For God's sake, Cyril. These people are criminals!"

The mayor made a tsk-tsk noise. "Why do we have to label people? I hate labeling people."

The mayor turned to Hob and nestled down in his chair. "I'm sure there's some middle ground we can agree on," he assured the boy. "But we cannot capitulate in our war on crime. I'd be voted out of office. . . . And I don't think anybody *wants* that."

Hob shrugged. "War on crime's okay with us. It's *business* we're talking about. You got any idea how many people *I* employ?"

"You know," the mayor conceded, "I've never thought about it that way. You're quite a . . . sharp kid."

Hob pointed a finger at the mayor. Kuzak leaned over the table, and Hob sneered at him. "You think I'm full of shit, don't you? Can't figure out how it is that I run things around here."

"I try to keep an open mind." The mayor smiled.

"Listen, dickhead," Hob said, his features growing hard. "They do what I tell them to do because they can't make NUKE without me. I'm the only one who knows the formula who isn't dead."

"He only saw it once," said Angie. "He's like that. Sees it and remembers it. Every detail."

"Photographic memory," added the mayor.

"Digital," Hob corrected. "So, your war on crime: You want to win it or what? We're the only chance you have."

"Say what?" Kuzak blurted.

Angie took that moment to plunge a NUKE ampule into her neck. "Lissen to him," she advised. "He has it all worked out."

"Why do people commit crime?" Hob asked.

"Well, most are . . ." The mayor hesitated. "Well, I guess because of drugs. Most people take drugs."

Hob shook his head. "Because they *want* drugs! The kind that *cost* too much. NUKE gives high quality at a cheap price, and if you get off our backs, we're gonna make it cheaper."

"And safer," Angie interjected.

"And safer," agreed Hob. "We don't shove our stuff down anybody's throat. We don't advertise, like they do with cigarettes and booze."

"Leave us alone," said Angie, "and anybody who wants it, gets it."

"So," concluded Hob, "no more crime. And you get to be the mayor who cleaned up Detroit."

Kuzak turned to an ashen-faced Poulos. "He's got a point."

The mayor next turned to the elderly lawyer. "Don't you think he has a point?"

The meeting was cut short by a screech of gears. The assembled stared at the side wall as, abruptly, it caved in, sunlight searing into their startled faces.

Silhouetted against the light and framed by the ruptured wall stood a hulking robotic shape. Eleven feet tall. Black as night. Angry as all hell.

Cain.

The beast cackled, sending a spine-chilling laugh throughout the building as he opened up with a burst of machine-gun fire that shattered the overhead lamp.

The conspirators tried to scramble out of the way. The metallic monster lit up its headlights, forcing the cowering crowd back further.

"God!" Poulos yelled. "What is that thing?"

The well-dressed hoods in the room pulled their guns and, lit by the blinding white light, opened fire. They were easily sliced in two by the steady rat-a-tat-tat gunfire offered by the Olympian intruder.

One hood, wielding an AK-47, fired a lethal round of fire at the gargantuan creature. The bullets pinged harmlessly off its king-sized chest. The thug hid behind the factory's boiler. A round of heavy-duty ammo slammed into the boiler, causing it to erupt into a wall of flame. Within seconds, the thug was nothing more than a quivering skeleton, its flesh melted upon the concrete flooring.

Hob dove under the table, his eyes wide with terror.

Angie ran to a corner and huddled amidst a mass of machinery. She pulled a NUKE ampule from her purse and tried to insert it into her neck. Her hand was shaking so hard she dropped it. "Damn!" she swore.

Kuzak and his followers crawled along the floor, passing the badly mauled bodies of mobsters.

Poulos and Thomas decided to make a run for it. The searchlight zeroed in on them.

Gunfire.

Thomas fell to the ground in six pieces.

Poulos threw up and hit the ground again as the searchlights passed above him. He skittered out of the factory and toward the mayor's limo.

Bullets zipped above his head, slamming into the limo and killing Corman, the driver.

Poulos leaped to his feet and began to run. He felt a shard of lead enter his back. He gaped down as his insides became outsides. He hit the side of the limo, dead.

Inside the battered factory, Angie cowered in a corner. She located another NUKE ampule and plunged it into her neck. Pfffft. Ahhhh. She felt better now. The lights wielded by the monster focused on her. She froze, her breath eluding her. The gigantic gorgon marched toward her, its body hissing and wooshing from its hydraulic system. The lights on her dimmed.

She gazed up at the black creature's head.

The visors atop the head sprang open.

She saw the ghostly face of Cain.

Angie stared at the visage in stoned-out disbelief

before grinning finally. "Cain! Oh, wow, man! You look great! Nice outfit!"

Angie walked toward the nightmare.

A large clawed hand reached out for her. She extended her right hand. "Really. It'll take some getting used to," she said, her speech slurred. "But it'll be *great*! Me and Hob, we'll always take care of you. . . . Just like always."

While Angie grabbed for the extended claw, the Cain-Creature's other hand reached behind her back and grabbed her by the throat, slowly and deliberately lifting her high off the ground.

Her garble ended in a gurgle.

The pincer grip tightened.

The decapitated thing that was once Angie dropped to the concrete floor. High above her, two metal slabs atop the monster's head snapped shut, effectively erasing the vision of Cain.

The monster turned its body, flaring its headlights to life.

Hob, still quivering in his pants under the table, gazed upward, tears in his eyes.

He scrambled as fast as he could toward the back of the armored truck filled with cash. Diving inside, he swung the heavy metal doors shut behind him.

He sat in the back of the truck sniveling.

He heard shotgun blasts outside.

One of Hob's well-dressed thugs opened up with a shotgun on the monster's back. The Cain-Creature swirled and dispatched the man with a shrug, turning the thug into something resembling pudding with a flick of its shoulder.

At the monster's feet, Mayor Kuzak crawled to a grated sewer opening.

The Cain-Creature next stared at the armored truck. Heaving its torso, it unleashed all its weaponry on the back of the truck, which began to collapse.

The Cain-Creature caught a glimmer of movement to its left. Kuzak was straining to lift the drainage grate above the sewer. He froze for a moment as floodlights lit the floor around him. Then, screaming, Kuzak tore off the grating and dropped into the sewer system as the monster above him raked the floor with bullets.

The mayor plunged into the sewer, splashing into the black muck. Kuzak didn't want to consider the origins of the dark water as bullets sliced deep into the sewer system. He knew what the Detroit River was made of these days.

He began to trot forward. Shit. He'd rather die of cancer than a bullet through his head. Somebody could *always* cure cancer.

A mile away, a solitary RoboCop guided his TurboCruiser through traffic. Thinking about the life he had left. Thinking about the life he might have recovered. Thinking about the world he had just given away, a victim of blackmail.

His ComLink buzzed to life on his dash. "Unit seventeen, we've got *heavy gunfire* at Cadillac Avenue and Toyota-Ford Expressway. No back-up available. Restricted area. Proceed at own risk."

Robo nodded toward the ComLink. "Got it. I'm on my way."

Robo had no idea, but he was about to meet and

witness the doings of his brother in OCP experimentations.

A big brother.

A big brother named Cain.

28

Robo drove his cruiser, its motor purring, onto the grounds of the battered factory. He pulled to a stop behind the mayor's shattered limo. Its roof was crushed. The driver, a bloodied mass, hung from his shattered window. Robo marched past the body of Councilman Poulos, unaware of what he would find inside the edifice.

He walked up to the ruptured wall and paused.

Inside the factory, Hob was pinned down by searchlights. His thin young body was cradled by fallen money. He was twitching spasmodically, and his eyes were wide in terror known only to very little boys.

He faced the lights, sure that it was Cain, returned to kill him.

"Nooooo!" he shrieked.

RoboCop entered the rear of the truck. Hob relaxed. Relaxed a lot. "Hiya," Hob whined.

"Hello." Robo nodded.

Hob glanced at the carnage around him. "This really sucks."

Robo knelt down next to Hob. The boy was trembling, fighting to stay conscious. He grabbed at Robo.

Robo embraced the fallen boy. "You are going into shock," he announced. "Try to stay calm. I will call for emergency medical teams."

"No!" Hob exclaimed. "Please! Don't leave me. I'm scared. It's really cold. Don't leave me!"

Robo stared at the boy.

Jimmy?

Son?

No.

He shook his head clear and said, evenly, "I will not leave you . . . son."

Hob almost managed a childish smile. "Thanks."

"What happened here?" Robo asked.

"I had this big deal going," the boy wheezed. "Then, *it* showed up."

"It?"

"Big. A mechanical man. Real big. Bigger than you."

Hob grabbed Robo's left hand. His head tilted back as his eyes rolled. He shook his young senses clear for a brief second.

"I'm gonna die, ya know," he said, nodding toward his torso.

Robo gazed at the crimson patch below the boy's nipples. It was growing larger and larger. A pain surged up from within Robo. He pushed it back down. He was a machine, after all. Without rights. Without feelings.

"I'm gonna die," Hob repeated. "But, you know what that's like, doncha?"

Robo nodded sadly. "Yes . . . yes, I do."

Hob arched his back. Blood dribbled from his grimaced lips.

"This really *sucks*," he whispered again, before relaxing his back. Before staring emptily into space.

Robo emitted a noise that sounded suspiciously like a sob.

He picked up the boy and cradled him in his arms.

Damn this world, he thought. Damn it to hell.

29

Casey Wong and Jess Perkins were on the tube, exchanging tattooed grins.

A film clip began behind Casey. A sheik, be-decked in his robes, and a dour Israeli prime minister faced off across a bargaining table.

"Israeli Prime Minister Yadir has flatly rejected the United Arab Emirate's latest offer of six trillion dollars for the Holy Land," Casey intoned. "While negotiations continue, each side maintains that their differences are strictly ideological."

The background switched to a crime scene, show-ing police guarding several pyramids of blood-stained money.

"And . . . it's *big money*," Jess chirped, "in local news as well. . . . An estimated five hundred million dollars in cash was confiscated today, but the state district attorney won't let the bankrupt city government touch it."

The bullet-riddled bodies of Poulos and Thomas appeared on the screen.

"Yes," Jess pointed out, "it's NUKE money,

seized at the sight of a massacre. Among the victims: Councilman Poulos and city attorney Darren Thomas. Was the city striking a deal with drug lords, hmmmmm? Mayor Kuzak?"

The scene switched to a perpetually flustered Mayor Cyril Kuzak facing a horde of reporters in front of City Hall. "These are men," he began, "who served our city so tirelessly. I won't comment on any of the charges. However, I make a promise to the people of Detroit: No effort will be spared to investigate this thoroughly."

The camera returned to a smiling Casey, who that night was trying especially hard to outdo the smiling Jess. "But," he said through his teeth, "there might not be time for an investigation. Not by the mayor's office, anyway. With the NUKE millions denied, the city has no hope of forestalling OCP's takeover of all city assets *tonight*."

The tube cut to a portrait of the Detroit Civic Centrum, a sleek, hundred-story skyscraper.

Casey stuck his head into the picture. "OCP has invited the media to attend the ceremony at the new Civic Centrum, when they officially take Detroit private."

Jess giggled. "Ought to be quite a bash! See you there, Casey."

"See you *all* there, Jess," Casey said, almost losing his eye contact with the camera.

A metal hand switched off the television.

Robo sat in silence.

He had things to do.

30

With Lewis at his side, Robo aimed his cruiser toward the entrance to OCP. He slammed the car to a halt. Robo and Lewis leaped out.

As they reached the building, a recently cleaned ED209 lumbered up to them, looking a bit like a well-honed Mr. Potatohead, but with minicannons in each hand.

The ED209 barked, "You are carrying firearms. Please present proof of authorization. You have ten seconds to comply."

The oversized egghead continued to lumber toward the pair.

"You now have five seconds to comply," it announced.

Lewis smiled at the tomato on stilts. "Knock it off," she chirped.

"Thank you for your cooperation," the robot said, before turning its back on them.

"I can't believe they're still making those stupid pieces of shit," Lewis muttered, marching alongside Robo toward the front entrance.

"That is the least of our problems," Robo hissed, bursting through the two front doors.

"Uh-oh," said Lewis. "I guess we're not playing this one by the book."

"The only book I recall is the Bible," Robo offered.

"Good one," Lewis said, scurrying after him. "But I think I forget the ending. As I recall, one of the two versions was a pretty bad scene."

Upstairs, in her office's private washroom, Dr. Faxx was taking great pride and pleasure in adjusting her makeup. She chatted soothingly into a cellular squawk-box at her side. "Yes, darling. The meeting ran a little long. The *general* does love to hear himself talk . . . and . . . talk and talk and talk. Ahahaha. Yes, I'll be right along. Bye."

Her assistant, Jenny, walked tentatively into the washroom.

"What is it?" Faxx glared at her.

Jenny tried to get her lips to work. "I'm sorry to bother you, but . . . Mr. Schenck just called from the lab. It's RoboCop!"

Faxx emitted a sound that only could be compared to a feline hiss and barged out of her office, her stiletto heels sparking along the tiled hallway floors.

"Sonofabitch artifact!" she swore, as an alarm system wailed to life above her.

She burst into the robotics lab, striding past several security guards who lay sprawled unconscious on the floor.

A computerized voice burped above her: "Alert! Security breach on level three."

She found Schenck cowering before the police officers. "This is private property! You're breaking the law."

Robo stood before her at a computer console. Lewis, her gun drawn, was at his side. Schenck whirled to face Faxx. "He's breaking the law!"

Lewis walked forward. "Yeah, he's full of surprises today."

She turned her attention to Faxx. "You want something?"

"What's the meaning of this?" Faxx fumed.

Robo flexed the access strip out of his clenched fist and plunged it into the lab's computer.

Lewis smiled sweetly. "Seems we got this killer robot on our hands. Couldn't think of a better place to start the investigation."

"I assume you have a warrant," Faxx sneered.

"Those banks contain classified data," Schenck whined. "There'll be charges."

The computer bank lit up with varied lights.

Schenck emitted a hoarse laugh. "You'll never break through the security code, Robo. I wrote it myself."

Robo twisted his spike. The data began to unscramble.

"My *God*! You can't!" Schenck amended. "This is impossible!"

"Stop him!" Faxx growled.

Schenck ran toward a keyboard and began tapping in signals. Robo glanced at him impassively. He slightly twisted his access spike. At Schenck's monitor, a video-game image, Nintendo-style, of RoboCop appeared. The computerized cop raised his pistol and fired. A cartoon explosion filled Schenck's screen. The words "BACK OFF, FAT-HEAD" appeared on the screen.

Schenck did as he was ordered.

"GAME ENDED" flashed on the startled scientist's screen.

In the distance, clanking footsteps echoed.

Lewis ran to the doorway, glancing over her shoulder at Robo. "It's okay. I'll handle it."

She ran out into the lobby to face a wobbly ED209. "Do not move," the titanic turd-head announced. "I am authorized to use lethal force."

Lewis sighed. This was old hat. She ran between the tater-topped mammoth's legs. The ED209 tracked her, trying to aim between its own legs. The outmoded robotic critter toppled forward and crashed to the ground with a resounding whooooof.

The thing lay on its back, mewing like a kitten.

"Pathetic!" Lewis sighed, striding back into the lab.

Inside, Robo was still plugged into the data banks. He consumed the weapons diagrams, the feeding mechanisms, the guts of Cain's workings.

Robo turned to Faxx and Schenck. "This is *Cain*!" he snarled.

Lewis stared at the two scientists. "Are you crazy? You bastards! You fucking crazy bastards!"

Robo twisted his data spike again. He removed the spike and turned to leave the room. Schenck's body trembled as he realized that all his data had been erased from the computer system.

"No!" he whined. "You've erased the whole file! You can't do this to me!"

Robo offered a salute. "I just did!" He marched toward the exit door.

Faxx ran after him. "Count your last hours, asshole. This is just the excuse we need. We're turning you off. You've been *replaced*! You're *obsolete*! You're an *embarrassment*!"

Robo glanced over his shoulder, almost a grin on his face. "Try me," he announced.

31

At the newly constructed Civic Centrum, a gala fete was taking place. Citizens of the city, not used to a celebration, clustered behind police barricades. Reporters surged around the front of the building.

Spotlights reflected off the front of the massive building, searching on into the heavens.

Jess Perkins, microphone in hand, smiled at the cameras. "Citizens interviewed on the scene express the excitement and the hope that OCP will make good on its promise of 'making life better in the Motor City.'"

A black limo purred up to the entrance of the building.

Johnson and the Old Man emerged, fighting off the horde of reporters.

The pressmen peppered them with questions.

"Does OCP own the city?"

"Will you hold elections?"

"Does this make us all OCP employees?"

"Isn't this a deliberate attempt to humiliate the mayor?"

Jess Perkins nudged her way forward. "Why aren't you going to City Hall?"

The Old Man said nothing, his smile blazing radiantly against the skyline of Detroit in the background. He suddenly turned to Jess. "Just a minute," he announced. "I'll answer that, young lady. City Hall is a decaying symbol of mismanagement and corruption."

A spotlight on the Centrum, as if on cue, illuminated the OCP logo on its facade.

"This magnificent structure," the Old Man continued, "OCP's Civic Centrum, is our gift to this *new* city."

Beyond the cluster of reporters, Mayor Kuzak's limo was approaching the centrum unnoticed.

The Old Man was feeling talkative. "This new seat of leadership for Detroit is our gift to our citizens," he said, beaming. "What better place for a new start?"

Kuzak sat in the back of his limo sullenly, watching the goings-on via his limo TV. He glanced toward a new speechwriter, barely out of college. The twit was typing on a laptop computer.

Kuzak sighed. "'A new start,'" he fumed. "I'll give that old fart a new start—right out of town. OCP will be drowned in a wave of populist sentiment. How's that speech coming?"

"Almost there," the twerp responded.

The limo screeched to a halt, sending Kuzak bolting forward. "What the hell—"

A dozen OCP guards flanked the limo.

"What the hell do you think you're doing!" Kuzak demanded.

"Please proceed to parking lot three. That's three blocks down Liberty, on the left," the first guard advised Kuzak, Jack Webb style.

"There's been a mistake!" Kuzak declared. "I'm the goddamned mayor!"

The guard pointed to a space on the horizon. "Sorry, sir. Media only. Your space is reserved. Three blocks down."

Kuzak eased himself back into the limo as the driver assumed his new course. The mayor faced the typing twerp. "Can you believe this shit? I'm the mayor and I can't get a parking space within three blocks!"

"Right," the typist enthused. "I got it."

"No!" Kuzak bellowed. "I don't want that in my speech!"

A cameraman ran up to the limo. Kuzak flashed an insipid smile as the limo pulled away.

Inside the monolithic structure the Old Man stood at a podium worthy of Mussolini, facing the multitudes, both live and via a hundred TV cameras.

"And, so," he said, "my dear friends, in a few moments OmniConsumerProducts and the troubled city of Detroit will join in a bold new enterprise."

Faxx ran into the room.

The Old Man pulled back a curtain. "I'd like to show you exactly what this will mean to you!"

The air was electric.

The curtains began to swing open, and the Old Man beamed at the assembled crowd. "Sometimes you just have to start over . . . right from scratch . . . to make things right. And that's *exactly* what we're going to do. We're going to build a *brand new city* where Detroit now stands."

A nearby band bleated out a fanfare.

The curtains finally swung apart.

There, on the stage behind the Old Man, stood a large-scale model of the Detroit of the future, hundred-story spires standing six feet high. It was sleek. Futuristic. Impressive. The Old Man marched before it, gesturing.

"This is my example to the world," he intoned. "Welcome to our city as it should be . . . and will be . . . in the hands of responsible private enterprise."

Flashbulbs went off. Cameras whirled. The assembled crowd gasped. Kuzak found himself escorted into the back of the room by a surly security guard. "Fuggoff," the mayor grumbled.

"And a special welcome to the mayor and the outgoing administration," the Old Man announced.

"We ain't goin' anywhere!" Kuzak shouted from the back of the room.

Kuzak was forced to the stage with his speechwriter by a burly guard. The Old Man extended a hand, but Kuzak glared at it.

"Your Honor," said the Old Man with a grin.

Kuzak glared at the model city and faced the microphones. "You'll have to tear down a lot of people's *houses* before you make that thing. Take away their *homes!*"

"Only to build sparkling, secure living units," the Old Man replied. "Now, please, take your seat on the stage."

"Won't be much room for *neighborhoods*," Kuzak pointed out. "The kinds we all grew up in."

"These days the neighborhoods just seem to be places where bad things happen," the Old Man argued. "Please, don't be so nostalgic."

"What about *democracy*?" Kuzak shouted. "Nobody elected you!"

"Anyone can buy OCP stock"—the Old Man smiled—"and own a piece of the city. What could be more democratic than that?"

Kuzak whirled toward the cameras. "That's bullshit! The people won't *stand* for this!"

"You haven't been following the polls." The Old Man sighed. "Please sit down."

Kuzak sank into a chair, and the Old Man smiled at the multitudes. "About a year ago, we gave this city RoboCop. Now, I think he's worked out pretty well, but things have gotten a little rougher out there. And now we need a law-enforcement unit capable of meeting the enemy on his own ground . . . and carrying enough firepower to get the job done."

The Old Man gestured behind him.

A hulking shape appeared behind the model of the gleaming, futuristic Detroit cityscape.

The crowd gasped.

The room was filled with a steady hydraulic hiss as the massive Cain-Creature lumbered forth.

"Ladies and gentlemen," the Old Man enthused, "I give you, with great pride . . . RoboCop 2!"

The Old Man found Faxx on the sidelines and smiled.

Faxx returned the smile nervously.

The hulking mechanical monster marched forward, taking Mayor Kuzak by surprise. "Those bastards," he muttered. "Those maniacs. Those killers."

"Something wrong?" the speechwriter asked.

"I can't believe this shit," the mayor mumbled. "These people are butchers!"

The mechanical monster flexed its body like a well-oiled tank truck as the crowd gasped. The Old Man grinned triumphantly. "He'll work twenty-four hours a day, seven days a week. There's going to be a big demand for this unit all across the country, and we'll make him right here in Detroit. That means *jobs* we can all be proud of. We're going to make 'Made in America' *mean* something again."

He turned to the mayor. "Shall we talk about what *your* leadership has brought us, Your Honor? Shall we take a look at the 'growth industry' *your* administration has made possible?"

The Old Man picked up a silver canister from under his podium and held it up. "This single container holds enough NUKE to addict a city block. A hundred of these are produced every day!"

He pushed a button on the side of the canister. It popped open, chock-full of NUKE ampules.

"These things are sent to the sweatshops where urban slaves prepare this poison for consumption by our friends, our loved ones, our children. I say this has got to stop. I say it's high time we brought an end to this man-made plague! RoboCop 2 will seek out every lab, every dealer, and *rid* our city of NUKE once and for all."

The Cain-Creature's head pivoted toward the

canister, suddenly alert. The Old Man didn't notice.

"Yes, things will be a lot quieter with this new boy around."

The metallic monster suddenly let out a howl. Its head flaps yanked open, revealing the hungry face of Cain. It reached a large talon down toward the canister. Startled, the Old Man held on tightly to the metal case, engaging in a brief tug-of-war.

The Old Man gasped. "What are you doing, son?"

"Fuck you!" The Cain-Creature roared again, snatching the canister in a jerking move and sending the ampules scattering in every direction.

The crowd, thinking it a gag, laughed.

The cyborg raised an angry fist, bellowing in frustration. The monster's head scanned the crowd angrily, its torso whirling. The Old Man backed away nervously. Faxx ran up to him. The Old Man grasped Faxx by the shoulders and shook her hard.

"Why is he doing this?" he demanded. "What's wrong with him?"

"The NUKE!" Faxx gasped. "Oh, God!"

"What?" the Old Man sputtered.

Faxx blanched. "Nothing. It's nothing."

The monster screeched and began smashing the model skyscape with a slashing motion of its mighty arms. It stepped forward, pulverizing model buildings beneath large pincered feet.

"I think you'd better turn it *off*!" the Old Man screamed at Faxx.

"I can't." Faxx smiled lamely. "But it's all right. It'll be all right."

The monster continued to smash the city of the future as video cameras recorded the entire debacle. OCP guards ran forward, training their automatic weapons on the berserk beast.

Faxx ran across the stage, spotting the weaponry. "Don't shoot!" she screeched. "It's not armed! It's *harmless!*"

Faxx fingered the control device as, behind her, the Cain-Creature roared at the guards. She punched every command she could muster.

The monster moved forward, bellowing down at her. Faxx whirled and dropped the control module, sending it clattering across the stage.

She screamed as the monster lunged at her.

Before it could cleave her in two, it stopped. A loud bang. A shell burst off the back of its neck. The monster pivoted, turning to the back of the stage, unharmed but angry.

There stood RoboCop, wielding a Cobra assault cannon.

The monster raised its machine-gun-laden arm. The firing mechanism of the gun snapped back and targeted Robo. Blutttepepep.

The monster gazed down. The gun wasn't loaded.

Robo fired the Cobra again.

The round burst harmlessly across the startled creature's chest.

The monster roared, stomping its foot and crashing into the stage with a resounding whaaap. It spotted the discarded command module and, reaching down, snatched it, punching in the command "ARM."

The Cain-Creature cackled as it raised its loaded arm. It blasted away at anything and everything that moved, tearing away chairs and slabs of wall.

Robo hit the floor in a daring roll-and-tuck maneuver, raising the Cobra high as the monster continued its firing frenzy.

The monster whirled toward Robo just as the supercop was about to fire. The Cain-Creature sent a round slamming into the Cobra, completely imploding the weapon before Robo had a chance to squeeze the trigger.

Robo slammed back into a wall, his hands twitching, his chest smoking.

He was hurt.

Hurt badly.

He tried to reach for his pistol. His fingers convulsed.

At that moment, the OCP guards opened up on the marauding metal monster. The Cain-Creature whirled around, firing all weapons on the galloping guards. Guards, guests, and TV reporters collapsed in the stream of screaming, seething, simmering lead pellets. Cameras exploded. Lights blew out.

The Cain-Creature cackled from within the computerized head. It turned its attention once again on Robo. It raised its taloned feet and wobbled toward him.

Robo shook his head clear, trying to get his system in synch with his RoboVision. Beneath his visor, he targeted the creature. He zoomed in on the barrel of the creature's massive cannon. TARGETING, his sensors told him. The Cain-Creature raised its lethal arm.

Robo winced and pounded out round after round. The monster's extended arm exploded.

The creature was caught by surprise. It howled at the heavens.

It continued to march forward, its shoulder gun and other weapons firing wildly. It was angry now. Out for blood. Out for vengeance. It hadn't chosen to be like this. It would kill everyone who kept it from controlling the world. Control. It had dreams. It had dreams of the future. World dominance. Universal submission for these poor human slugs.

The scooping ram shot out from its arm, sending a grappling tentacle toward Robo.

Robo tried to dodge it, but the tentacle slammed into him, sending Robo crashing through a wall and into a hallway. Robo scrambled down the hallway, avoiding the still-pursuing tentacle.

There were times he wished he wasn't a cop.

Murphy gasped as he trotted down the hallway.

Murphy, Robo considered. *Murphy. I am Alex J. Murphy. A fighting Irishman, you percolating piece of metal.* His legs pumped harder.

Outside the building, an army of police converged, their TurboCruiser sirens wailing.

Lewis, Stef, and Whittaker led the charge inside the building, Stef bellowing over a megaphone, "Clear the area! You are all in danger!"

Inside, Robo continued to elude the tentacle. By this time, the Cain-Creature was marching after him, tearing through walls and crashing through corridors.

Robo jumped through the gate of a large freight elevator, frantically pushing buttons.

Nothing happened.

Robo reached up and punched a metallic hand

through the wall of the elevator car, pulling himself up and over the car on its main cable. Sitting above the car and hanging on the cable, Robo pulled the high voltage cable in two, leaving just enough tethers intact to keep the elevator in place.

The monster approached the elevator, not firing, relishing the kill.

Robo stood immobile above the car.

The monster crouched to enter the elevator, Cain's face grinning on its head monitor.

It lurched upward toward the hiding RoboCop.

Robo ducked and extended the sparking, high-voltage cable.

The monster grasped the cable and was thrown back.

Robo severed the cable, his body jerked high into the air as the cable snapped.

The Cain-Creature, caught by surprise, was tossed to the top of the elevator car as it plunged downward, floor after floor, due to lack of a main cable.

As the monster descended, pulling the severed cable down with it, Robo found himself hanging onto the main cable, yanked upward story after story, the snapping, flapping cable twisting and turning in his hand.

With a resounding crash, Robo was thrust into the elevator's gears at the very top of the complex's elevator shaft. His arms plunged deep into the gears.

He heard the falling elevator with the Cain-Creature aboard crash at the bottom of the shaft below.

Robo heaved a sigh of relief, but then he heard a curious scraping sound.

He glanced downward.

The metallic monster had survived the crash and now, using its talons, was slowly climbing up the shaft.

Up the shaft to where Robo hung helplessly.

The Cain-Creature began to pick up speed, digging into the metal shaft faster and faster, like an old-time locomotive picking up speed.

Robo wrenched his arm from the elevator mechanism and sent his body plummeting feetfirst toward the advancing mechanical madman.

Glancing upward, the Cain-Creature tried to halt its advancing body's progress. Too late. Robo's feet slammed into its head mechanism, causing it to lurch violently to the side.

The two went crashing through the towering building's side.

Outside.

Space. Nothing but space. A starlit night. A sheer drop of ten stories.

The metal monster dug its claws into the side of the building. Below it, ant-sized police cruisers. A tiny crowd. A fall meaning certain death.

Robo slid down the monster's spine, grabbing hold of its legs.

Robo, the creature's legs clutched to his bosom, braced his own legs against the building's side.

"It's all over, Cain," he stated. "We're going down. We're going down together."

The monster growled as its steel pincers began to sag downward.

Sparks arose as metal met metal, the creature clawing at the side of the newly constructed high-rise.

"Damn you!" Robo said, pushing his feet forward against the building, swinging the creature's bottom out toward the heavens.

The Cain-Creature howled as it lost its grip.

RoboCop and RoboCop 2, his scientifically created brother named Cain, plunged toward the streets below.

The stars watched in silence.

The crowds below gasped in unison.

Silhouetted against the sky, two metal figures fell.

The only sound to be heard was the hiss of metal against a damp Detroit evening.

The hiss grew to a shriek. The sound of a falling bomb.

The crowd below backed away. Lewis stood next to her cruiser, watching the tangle of metal descend to the ground.

She raised a pallid hand to her mouth. "Murphy!" she whispered. "Oh, my god! Oh no! No!"

The shrieking sound grew louder as the metal mass drew closer to the ground. Cameramen trained their lenses while reporters clutched their ears.

In the air, the computerized Cain-face screeched.

Robo grit his teeth and stared stolidly at the approaching street.

Robo extended an arm.

He caught hold of a window, sending both metallic creations swinging into the building.

The falling metal mass careened inside the skyscraper, sending startled workers vaulting from their workplaces. Ceilings exploded and walls caved in.

Robo continued to clutch at the tumbling metallic monster as the Cain-Creature thrashed at him.

Below, at the entrance to the building, police and OCP guards erected barricades as, above them, the two metal creations continued to flail against each other, smashing through the side of the building and tumbling onto the overpass. Robo and the monster slammed their fists at each other, causing their bodies to smash through the overpass and down onto the street below.

The metal mass crashed through the roof of a newly constructed parking garage, flattening a station wagon.

The weight of their combined bodies forced them down through the ground-level floor of the parking edifice, where they landed with a crunching thud.

Robo continued to work over the Cain-Creature. The massive metal monster continued to writhe. They rolled through large, expansive causeways of pipe. They smashed through warning signs reading "DANGER: GAS MAIN."

The floor shook.

The walls collapsed.

The monster clawed at Robo's helmet. Robo stiffened as electrical charges caressed his skull.

The monster got to its feet, sending Robo smashing into a cellar wall.

The monster grabbed a limp RoboCop and hurled him into a gas main.

222

The Cain-Creature cackled, releasing a small vestigial arm. A cutting torch snapped from its claw, stabbing at Robo's visor. Robo attempted to roll his way out of the snapping claws of the eleven-foot snapping, snarling creature.

The torch neared Robo's eyes. Robo extended both battered hands, grabbing the torch and twisting it.

The Cain-Creature roared in anger as Robo thrust the torch into the nearby gas main.

Robo twisted his head to watch the torch tip smack into the main.

A fireball whooooshed forward.

Robo lost his vision.

Outside, both police and civilians ran as a tremendous fireball smashed its way through the base of the building.

Blast after blast erupted from the bowels of the building.

Lewis began to scream.

Fire and smoke were all around her.

Behind her, sirens screamed to the scene.

A fireball erupted from a street grate near her.

Abruptly, the fireball disappeared.

A charred hand grabbed the grate and pushed it upward.

Robo emerged intact. He got to his feet, wobbled, and, facing Lewis, collapsed face-first onto the ground. Lewis ran toward him while, from the bottom of the building, the badly damaged Cain-Creature lumbered forward.

Both police and OCP guards opened fire on it.

The creature whirled dizzily, opening up its

weaponry on its assailants, sending a dozen men to the ground, all dead.

In the crowd, Ellen Murphy, gathered with her neighbors to watch the salvation of her city, threw herself down on top of her son, Jimmy.

A police cruiser exploded, sending a fiery arm of smoke and debris toward the sky.

On a balcony overlooking the debacle, the Old Man stood immobile. He turned to a sweaty Johnson. "This could look bad for OCP, Johnson. Scramble the best spin team we have. We have to outdistance ourselves from this in terms of public relations."

"Gotcha," Johnson said, scurrying off.

Down below, the monster raged. Lewis, turning from the fractured Robo, spotted an abandoned armored patrol vehicle. She climbed into the truck's cab.

The creature continued to fire on the crowd, killing both civilians and cops alike. Stef caught a slug in the forehead, his brains blowing out his skull. He fell into a startled Whittaker's arms.

"Awww, Stef," Whittaker moaned, easing his fallen comrade's body to the ground before raising his own weapon again and firing a salvo at the berserk beast.

The monster whirled, stopping its fire, as a siren approached.

Lewis, at the wheel of an armored police truck, grinned grimly as she sped toward the titan.

The monster roared and blasted the car with machine-gun fire.

Lewis crouched down behind the wheel as bullets

pinged around her. "Fuck you, Frankenstein!" she yelled, as the truck slammed into the guts of the monster.

The truck embedded itself in the creature.

The monster shot off a few minimissiles, blowing up two cruisers. Cops and civilians ran for dear life.

Lewis, stuck in the cab embedded in the writhing beast, kicked open the driver's door and threw herself to the ground.

The creature grabbed the truck from its innards and sent it hurling to the ground with a deafening crash. The vehicle exploded.

The monster cackled, blinded by the flames.

Beneath the flame and smoke, RoboCop crawled toward the Cain-Creature.

Lewis ran to Robo's side. "There's no stopping that thing, Murphy! Your plan won't work!"

Robo grimaced at her. "It's the only way. Get into position."

Lewis nodded and darted off.

The monster burst forth from behind the flames, scanning the area and sniffing.

From behind a wall of smoke, Robo strode, a gnarled truck before him.

The monster fired a salvo at Robo, hitting the truck instead.

The monster charged forward. It skidded to a stop, focusing on the truck.

A hand appeared before the battered vehicle: Lewis's hand, holding a canister of NUKE.

The Cain-Creature zeroed in on it and stopped firing its weaponry.

Lewis emerged from behind the truck. "It's

NUKE, Cain. A lot of NUKE. It's all *yours*. Come on. You want it, Cain?"

The Cain-Creature's chest-emplaced feeding mechanism opened. It lurched toward Lewis.

"Yeah," she called, holding the metal canister. "You're really hurting. You really want it. Come on, bullet-head."

The monster clanked toward Lewis. Within seconds, it towered over her.

"That's right," she encouraged. "It's all yours."

The monster reached for the canister. As it did so, Lewis heaved it high into the air. The Cain-Creature gasped as the canister soared into the sky, end over end. Lewis darted away from the metal monster, taking cover behind a cruiser. The monster extended its tendril, pulling the canister toward its feeding mechanism and turning its back on all concerned.

Robo leaped upon the ignored, abandoned truck. He launched himself into space.

He landed on the creature's back.

The monster, sensing the intrusion while imbibing the drug, thrashed around. He attempted to fire his shoulder gun, but he couldn't manage to target Robo.

Lewis watched the battle. "A monkey on his back," she whispered. "That's what you said would bring him down, Murphy. Christ, I hope you're right."

The monster tried to grasp at Robo from its shoulders. One claw sliced into Robo's neck and fluid spurted. The Cain-Creature's claw cut deeper.

Robo found himself screaming.

He was dying.

Robo called up his RoboVision. On his visor read: "SYSTEMS DAMAGE ALERT: EFFICIENCY 44%."

The creature sent its cutting torch toward Robo, who grabbed it with his free hand, twisting it with all his might. He ripped the torch off the monster's body with a shower of sparks.

The monster went berserk, bucking like a bronco, Robo on its back.

Robo tugged at the protective plate on the monster's spine.

The monster reared back, slamming Robo into the side of a streetlamp. The lamp crumbled. Robo nearly did as well. Yet he continued to hold on.

The protective plate on the monster's back flew free. Robo forced his hand into the back of the monster's main circuitry.

The creature dropped to all fours, bucking back and forth like a stubborn mule. Robo continued to hold on, his feet flying high into the air.

Robo pounded his fists into the circuitry.

A sudden flash erupted from the back of the Cain-Creature's head.

Simultaneously, the creature sent a crab-claw smacking deeper into Robo's head. Essential fluid gushed from Robo's battered body.

Robo screamed.

The monster howled.

It was down to this, now. Brother against brother. Experiment against experiment.

Robo thought of the children.

THE CHILDREN.

THE FUTURE.

Robo emitted a howl and plunged his hand into the back of the monster's head, yanking out wiring and circuitry and bits and pieces of a human brain and nervous tissue.

Robo felt a surge of electricity snap on his extended hand.

He tried to yell.

His voice emerged as nothing more than a gurgle. "Good-bye," he whispered. *For the children,* he thought.

Robo tumbled from the monster's back, landing in a heap and passing out. *For the children* was his last thought.

He raised his left hand and brought what was left of Cain's human brain down onto the pavement with a *splat*.

His eyes closed as the Cain-Creature sputtered, stammered, spat, and slumped. The monster collapsed onto the street with a teeth-gnashing shriek.

A crowd of police and onlookers ran forward, ambulances screaming in the distance.

High above the scene, from a top floor, the Old Man surveyed the scene, very unhappy. Next to him stood Johnson and OCP attorney Holzgang.

Holzgang sighed. "Of course, there will be a rash of civil suits, wrongful deaths, injuries, destruction of property."

"That's just money," the Old Man replied. "What about criminal proceedings?"

"I'm sure that major indictments will be raised against all parties responsible."

"That means *me!*" the Old Man spat.

The lawyer remained silent. The Old Man digested that.

Johnson perked up. "What if this were all the work of one individual? A person who had her own agenda that was not in synch with the goals of our company?"

The Old Man glanced at Johnson as the young executive went on. "A woman who was not a team player? Who violated our trust?"

The Old Man nodded, considering this. "Of course," he offered, "we'd need evidence to support that."

"Sir," said Johnson, beaming, "whether it exists or not, I know we can find it."

The Old Man returned the smile. "I'm sure you can. I'm sure you *will*, Johnson."

"Yessir."

At that moment, Dr. Faxx staggered into the room, staring imploringly at the Old Man. She ran to him, embracing him.

"Oh, God!" she said. "It was so horrible. I thought it was going to kill me."

The Old Man stared over her head. "Yes, but it's over now, Juliette. All over."

He looked at Johnson. "You have work to do. Better get to it right away."

Johnson nodded and, grinning, left the room. "Yessir."

On the streets below, the cleanup was winding down. Robo sat stunned in a corner, shaking his head from side to side. Lewis brought him his pistol.

"Some kid saw it on the sidewalk and tried to steal it."

Robo grasped the pistol and glanced upward.

Mayor Kuzak stood above him.

"This is a great day for·the Motor City, Robo," the mayor chirped.

Robo got to his feet to face Kuzak and a gaggle of reporters. Kuzak rushed to his side, wrapping an arm around him. "Thanks to the finest police officer this city has ever seen, the corruption of corporate greed has been thwarted."

Robo scanned the crowd before him. There, behind the reporters, was Ellen Murphy, with little Jimmy trying to get a good look at Robo.

Robo locked eyes with Jimmy.

He twirled his gun, just like Jimmy's TV hero, T. J. Lazer.

He twirled it a second time, adding a flourish to the move, before he slammed the gun back into his holster.

He saw Jimmy applaud.

The boy *knew*.

Jimmy *knew*.

He nodded his head toward the boy, before becoming aware of a tired Lewis leaning her body against his. She smiled at him. His hand silently slipped down to hers and squeezed it. Robo eyed the mayor, still jabbering away. "Detroit belongs to the people again. To *us*!"

Robo casually slipped his arm around Lewis's waist. She stared up at him, smiling but startled.

The mayor babbled ever onward. "And this guy here? He's a symbol! . . ."

Lewis began to chuckle at her own feelings as Robo's hand easily slid the pair of handcuffs off the belt around her waist.

"You idiot," she whispered.

Robo raised the handcuffs.

"Yes," the mayor intoned, "he's a *symbol*!"

"Nope," Robo said, smashing the handcuffs down upon the startled mayor's wrists.

He faced them both.

"I'm just a cop."

Lewis beamed at him. "A good cop."

Robo managed a grin.

That's all he ever wanted to be.

EPILOGUE

RoboCop sat silently in his TurboCruiser, looking at the dank, gray, night sky above him.

He tilted his head back.

He should be back at the stationhouse by now. He knew that. He should've been strapped into his throne with two robotics experts monitoring his impulses. Tonight, however, he didn't feel like it.

He stared at the sky and wondered.

Wondered what would happen to Ellen and Jimmy.

Wondered if Ellen really knew that Alex J. Murphy was alive and moderately well and living in an Olympian body made of metal and human tissue.

He wondered about Anne Lewis.

His partner.

Would she ever become more than just his partner?

Most of all, he wondered about himself.

Was he a man or a machine? If he was a man, he was a pretty darned hard one. If he was a machine, he was a pretty flawed one, brimming with emotions and shortcomings.

He flicked on the transmission and pressed his large foot to the accelerator.

He took a deep breath, sending his computerized innards whirring. Forget it, he thought. Let his insides blow a gasket or two. He managed to discern the scent of fresh night air.

He gunned the engine, sending the cruiser heading deep into the night.

Hell, he didn't care *what* he was.

He knew *who* he was.

Alex J. Murphy. A cop. The son of a cop.

And maybe, some day, the father of a cop.